Praise for *Exit Lane*

"I devoured *Exit Lane* in a single weekend and felt buzzy from the slow-burning sexual tension. It's the best of *When Harry Met Sally*, *Normal People*, and *Lady Bird* all wrapped up in a vintage button-down and sprinkled with Midwestern charm."

—Joanna Goddard, *Cup of Jo*

"Do you love flirting? Intense sexual tension rooted in authentic feeling? Loafers with old Levi's? You are going to stay up way past your bedtime devouring this novella."

—Molly Prentiss, author of *Tuesday Nights in 1980* and *Old Flame*

"Erika Veurink pulls off a fun, charming read with just enough scandalous young-people behavior to remind you that we are all a mess and that falling in love is a journey that's well worth the adventure and the many detours."

—Aminatou Sow, coauthor of the *New York Times* bestseller *Big Friendship*

"With *Exit Lane*, Erika Veurink has announced herself as an electrifying new presence in the world of romcom fiction. I've already read it twice."

—Caro Claire Burke, author of the forthcoming *Yesteryear*

Exit Lane

ERIKA VEURINK

831 STORIES

831 Stories

An imprint of Authors Equity
1123 Broadway, Suite 1008
New York, New York 10010

Copyright © 2025 by Erika Veurink
All rights reserved.

Cover design by C47
Book design by Scribe Inc.

This is a work of fiction. Names, characters, places and incidents either are products of the author's imagination or are used fictitiously.

Library of Congress Control Number: 2025937188
Print ISBN 9798893310610
Ebook ISBN 9798893310627

Printed in the United States of America
First printing

www.831stories.com
www.authorsequity.com

For my sister, Sarah, the first love of my life

I

MARIN

The sun streaks in through the slivers of window on either side of the air-conditioning unit, and it takes me a few waking moments to register the arm of my longtime on-again, off-again girlfriend draped across my chest.

As I gently lift her wrist, Georgie stirs with a devilish smile, bringing me right back to earth. "It's good luck to have sex on graduation day," she hums, kissing my face, my neck, my hip as she shimmies under the covers, armed with the vibrator she left charging the night before. I close my eyes and let my head fall back, trying to be present but feeling far away. Which is actually where I want to be.

When I finish and she comes up for air, I trace a constellation of freckles across her back. "I'll miss this," she says, rolling over into a sunspot on her pilled gray duvet.

"Me too," I say, and I mean it. It's hard to believe I came to the University of Iowa hoping people would think I was straight, worried being bisexual might be some kind of disappointment. But once I settled in—once I got over the novelty of being someone other than the girl with the dead dad—it felt like space opened up for something else.

The one-hour-and-fifty-five-minute drive felt far enough away from home to try on an identity that I thought might fit. Self-assured and up-for-anything Georgie, president of Chi Omega, social coordinator of the Pride Alliance Center, helped me find a rhythm, some kind of belonging. But as I kiss her goodbye, I feel a relief, an acknowledgment that my time here is over and that my real life can start.

On campus, parents are at Hy-Vee purchasing black-and-gold "Class of 2017" balloons, cases of Coors, and flimsy greeting cards to stuff with cash. My personal celebration is going to look more like driving a thousand miles and never turning back.

As I step out into the morning sun, rolling my shoulders back into a big stretch, I hear the band tuning its instruments to *Pomp and Circumstance* on the still-dewy turf of Kinnick Stadium. Beneath it, the sound of Sloane's voice as she answers my phone call: "Why are you up?" She responds with a question. Typical. I imagine her filling in the last of the Saturday crossword in pencil while sipping a responsible half cup of coffee. "God, I see you walking from the Chi O house. You think you're so original for getting laid our last morning of college." I wave to where I know my best friend is looking down from the living room we share. She's probably already dressed—like a future First Lady, as usual, a long brown ponytail hanging at the nape of her neck, as carefully constructed as the sculptures at the state fair butter-carving competition.

"Did Teddy confirm what time he could pick me up?" I ask as I cross the street.

"Yep, you're all set to leave at five."

EXIT LANE

"We can agree he's only doing this because he's desperately in love with you, right?"

She ignores me. "You don't have a car. You're both headed to New York. It just makes sense. But I *can* agree that it is remarkable that he's still willing to do this despite your unwillingness to just text him back directly to coordinate this whole thing. But I am, as ever, happy to act as your admin. I will sort of miss it when you have a real one." Ever logical, she has a way of finishing a sentence that annoys her opponents on the debate team and fills me with calm. She's the one part of my college experience I can't bear to think about leaving. Our plan is to reunite in the city eventually, but for now, we try to avoid the topic of our inevitable distance.

After our freshman year of dorm living, Sloane and I moved into a luxury building on the edge of campus. Though her parents assure me I pay half the rent, we all know my monthly check barely covers the co-op fee.

"Your gown is steamed in the bathroom," she says as soon as I step through the door and kick off my loafers. "There's extra turkey bacon in the oven. And when are you going to deal with your closet? You know, for someone who claims to love a plan . . ."

I reach for her shoulder, smiling, and pull her in for a hug. "I trust that you'll still be micromanaging my life long-distance."

I leave her to her own preparations and collapse, for the last time, onto my bed, a wrought-iron beauty I rescued from Craigslist and transformed with the aid of Sloane and a can of spray paint on the roof during finals. I only ruined one pair of pants.

3

I look around at everything that's still left to pack. Dad's funeral program tucked into the frame of a pink-and-black *Funny Face* poster. Macroeconomics textbooks I promised my Chi O little. A row of blue and white button-ups, some thrifted blazers. My beloved, pristine loafers, purchased after landing a competitive venture capital internship in New York. My heart rate rises in excitement as I process the gravity of the moment, and I fan my arms like a kid making a snow angel. The back of my throat goes dry, and I'm suddenly lightheaded from anticipation, hunger, or both. Today is the start of the promise I made myself when I was fifteen: that someday I would leave all of Iowa behind. I have two suitcases. Seven hours. And a triple espresso waiting for me in the kitchen.

TEDDY

"Graduation sex"—I barely get the words out, watching Emilie, an ex from freshman year, pulling on a heel at the foot of my bed—"is good sex, I mean, good luck." She smiles, grabs her keys off my dresser, and promises to add me on LinkedIn. I laugh to myself as I tug on my boxers.

After the door shuts, I know it's time to face the inevitable: I am moving out and moving on, even if a not-insubstantial part of me wishes my life in Iowa City could last forever—the house parties, the group projects I carried mostly on my own, the late nights in the library that turned into early mornings.

EXIT LANE

When I got accepted into the NYU School of Law, I briefly but seriously considered staying at Iowa instead. After working through a robust pros/cons chart on the whiteboard in my favorite study room in the business school, I knew what I had to do. I'd go learn everything I possibly could from a new place and new people, then bring it all back home. "We'll always be here," my mom reminded me. "Now's the time to spread your wings."

My eyes drift to a stack of cards sitting on top of my dresser: one for my sister Romy, one for my parents, and one for my childhood best friend and forever accomplice Carter. Notes thanking them for their support the past four years. Proof that learning to shotgun a beer hadn't murdered my manners.

I lean onto my elbow to open the disintegrating blinds, revealing crowds ambling toward the football field. "Amateur hour," I mutter. I'd reserved tickets for my and Carter's families weeks ago and booked an eight-person reservation for late lunch in town. Our combined family dinners used to be a weekly occurrence, most Sunday nights after football games or church, and the weight of this being the last time we'd all be together for a while was palpable. It was a pressure on my chest that kept me from moving to my feet.

I check my phone, fully charged on the windowsill where I leave it every evening, to find a drunk voicemail I convinced Carter to record for posterity at Donnelly's last night. Nostalgic already, I download it for safekeeping and scroll back to a text from Sloane, confirming plans for me to take someone named Marin with me when I depart for my drive to New York this afternoon. I hadn't planned on company, but how could I say no to the gorgeous, divinely aloof Sloane Bachman?

Three knocks interrupt thoughts of my entirely unrequited crush.

Carter. "Decent!" I shout toward the door, and he enters, balancing two sweating iced coffees in his hands and a bag of bagels under his chin.

"Ran into a very adorable ghost on the way in," he says, dropping the carbs at the foot of my bed with a tilt of his head. "Emilie? From Econ 101?" Carter's encyclopedic memory of my dating life is both endearing and creepy. Plied with enough drinks, he could recite every single one of my love interests since first grade.

I reach for my coffee with an eye roll. "I plead the fifth?"

He laughs. "You ready?"

"One sec." I text Sloane back—promptness equals points in her book—and finally bring my feet to the floor.

The ceremony is eternal, but not long enough. Our parents are waving from row 5, zooming in with their ancient iPhones, dabbing tears. A reminder that the moisture pooling in my own eyes is genetic hardwiring. After lunch, Carter and I both continue to cry in the Joseph's parking lot while our dads pretend to make small talk ten feet away and our moms hover, patting each other's shoulders and digging in their purses for another pack of tissues. Carter is headed to

Reno for a top-secret engineering job, and we've spent the last four months trying to pretend like the cross-country moves we're making aren't terrifying. That we have any idea how to navigate the world without each other. We hand each other our letters. "We're so cheesy," Carter jokes, stuffing my note in his pocket. "Obviously I can't read this now. I'm really going to miss you. Promise me you won't fall in love with some Upper East Side snob and never come back?"

I laugh and hug him hard. "It's just for now. We'll get married and have kids, and our kids will get married and have kids, and we'll hardly remember this." I say it in a joking tone, but he knows that I mean it. "Promise to save a spot for me on Fifty-First Street," I add more earnestly.

The plan has always been simple: Carter would live at 441 Fifty-First Street, Des Moines, Iowa, his grandparents' former address and the site of some of our best memories, and I would live in 443 Fifty-First Street next door. But for now, it's Nevada and New York and a shared commitment to call each other every Sunday.

I pull my late grandma's 1998 LeSabre out of the parking lot. The gas light flicks on, and the check engine light follows in short order. It's fine. What matters is getting to the meeting spot on time. In all likelihood, punctuality is Sloane's love language.

When I make the turn in front of the main library, I see them: Sloane, somehow still stoic despite tears streaming down her face, hugging a woman almost a foot taller than her—dark blond, terrifying, with a cigarette dangling from her lip and an *Annie Hall* outfit hanging off her frame. Sloane's in chinos, ballet flats, and a navy-and-white striped boatneck. Are those . . . printed-out directions in her hand? Her friend looks familiar, maybe from an elective or Young Democrats or something. I squint as I approach and pull the visor down.

Now that I have a better view, I can tell that the friend is beautiful—actually, stunning—with features that look like they could slice right through me, though a little too androgynous for my personal taste. Sloane's a gin and tonic after a long day of yard work. This woman—Marin— is a Negroni after a big meeting. *Not that I've ever had a long day of yard work or a big meeting*, I think. She intimidates me even from a distance, and yet her high cheekbones and arched eyebrows make my stomach tighten in a way I recognize. As I roll to a stop at the curb, I sit up straighter, checking for remnants of lunch in my teeth and tracking the way Marin's weight shifts from her front foot to her back, how she lifts her chin while forcing a smile.

The two of them pull apart and walk toward the Buick, where I hand-crank the passenger window open. Sloane turns on a smile, a real one I think, as she angles her stretched-out arms in a sideways V like she's unveiling a work of art. "Teddy, meet Marin."

Sixteen hours. How bad could it be? I reach over to extend a hand out the window.

"Hi, Teddy," she says, eyes narrowing. "Can you open the trunk?"

II

MARIN

"Thanks for doing this," Sloane says to Teddy while tossing me a Ziploc bag with my favorite yogurt-covered pretzels and the Altoids I chew whenever I'm restless. As he climbs out of the car, almost reluctantly, I take him in. His shirt collar is askew—I would fix it if I knew him—but his sneakers are clean, like he takes care of them. Teddy looks like most of the guys who have crushes on Sloane: charmingly unkempt light-brown hair; miraculously clear skin, despite a frat-boy diet; and a '90s rom-com always-gets-the-girl air. I've observed countless Teddy types trip over themselves to get Sloane a drink in a sweaty basement or leave grocery-store carnations at our apartment door.

He seems relaxed, considering we're both at the same precipice, and it unnerves me. The car suits him, which I consider mentioning as an insult but keep to myself. I can already hear Sloane's "What could you possibly mean by that?" He gives the impression he fantasizes about three-car garages and coaching a Little League team. There's a clear through line from his crush on her, the feat of American engineering he's driving, and the handwritten note I spot on the dash. Teddy's the dream my dad had for me as a little girl, a "happy wife, happy life" guy. He's everything I'm trying to run away from, wrapped in a striped rugby shirt that fits him better than it should.

As Teddy climbs back into the car, I hug Sloane one last time. I promise to call the second I get to my new home on East Eighty-Third Street—a parquet-floored two-bedroom apartment partitioned to accommodate my cousin, two of her theater friends, and now me. "There's no crying in baseball, Mar," she whispers, wiping the tears from both of our eyes. Our first Halloween together, we showed up to Donnelly's in matching skirted baseball uniforms, an homage to *A League of Their Own*. It was the first time we'd used our fake IDs, and memories of this truly inconsequential milestone make my throat feel tight.

Destabilized, I try to focus on one inhale, one exhale. Losing Sloane, or losing my proximity to Sloane, feels like a small death. And despite how avoidant we've been about this topic, it's been on my mind constantly.

I sink into the bucket seat, and she squeezes my hand. "Please take care of yourself. And try not to fall in love with Mr. All-American on the way to New York." We turn to look at Teddy, who is spitting sunflower seeds into a red plastic cup. Sloane raises her brows and shuts my door. It's going to be a long ride.

We pull out of the parking lot, waving longer than Sloane can see us, as if to say our goodbyes not just to her but to all of it, before we merge onto I-80 East.

"I figured we'd spend the night outside of Chicago and

EXIT LANE

finish the rest of the drive tomorrow," Teddy says, his voice confident but quieter than I expect. He holds the wheel with one hand and props his head against the other, his elbow lodged on the windowsill. His certainty could read as arrogance, but I sense it's just . . . him. I try to give him the benefit of the doubt, as someone whose directness also sometimes reads as conceitedness. The worn-in cotton of his purple-and-yellow rugby shirt tugs at his bicep, and my vantage point gives me a good angle on his jawline, sharp and angular. Maybe Sloane should reconsider his obvious affection for her.

"Works for me," I respond, ready to daydream in peace for a few hours, ideally to some music. "Do you mind if I turn on the radio?"

His eyes crinkle. "The radio's shot. The AC, too. I assumed Sloane told you." Nothing slips Sloane Bachman's mind, especially not details as damning as these. "Sorry, it's not exactly luxury travel." He smiles slightly, and his eyes land on me long enough for it to feel deliberate.

"I can rough it." I reach for my mints and turn my body toward the window.

I pictured my arrival in New York triumphant, or at least with modern amenities. There's nothing filmic about the situation I've found myself in, or the silence that's growing louder by the minute.

I lean back in the seat, watching the office parks and megachurches blur by. In an instant, I'm an eight-year-old in Sunday school, accepting salvation at the altar for the fifteenth time. I'm a ten-year-old trailing behind my dad at

Bring Your Child to Work Day, carrying a pocketbook full of business cards he printed with my name. I'm eighteen and hiding my acceptance letters to UC Berkeley and Columbia, convinced that picking a college near my sister is the most important thing. All these Marins belong here, in Iowa. I'm ready for the start of a new self in New York, one without the grief or the impossible weight of always doing it right.

Around Geneseo, Illinois, I decide I've heard enough of Teddy's sunflower seed spitting. The car's sticky, and I can see sweat drops gathering on his collarbone. I can't go on like this. "Let's play a game," I suggest with more enthusiasm than I actually feel. He looks at me, left arm draped out the open window. I catch a whiff of his scent—boy mixed with some cologne I can't identify but don't hate. Teddy's attractive, I decide, if you're into the life-of-the-party, whole milk, Iowa suburbs type. "Let's go back and forth and tell each other what we know to be true about the other person."

Teddy laughs, and it's the loudest sound I've heard him make so far. "This feels like freshman orientation. But I'm in. You start."

And suddenly, as he nods in my direction, it hits me. We've met before.

I sit up taller and run my eyes over him as my brain sifts through memories. The chill of football bleachers. The scent of corn during summers of detasseling. Teddy's somewhere, his face just out of recollection. "Oh my god." I laugh, a faint memory coming into focus in my mind. "You went to Valley High School, didn't you?" Of course:

EXIT LANE

Teddy McCarrel, whose little sister I played against in a tennis tournament senior year.

"Wait, are you from Des Moines?"

"I went to Sacred Heart. Plaid skirt and plastic babies for pro-life day."

His laughter joins my own. "Is it true about those kids getting caught having sex in the confessional? That shit was lore at Valley."

"Not only true, but not the first time. My dad always tried to tell people he was the first to do it in the '80s."

"Absolute legend. Please tell him I said so."

My face falls, and my instinct is to blame myself for initiating conversation, as if Teddy and I could ride like monks for the better part of two days. Lightheaded, I feel a familiar apprehension build: the one that precedes dropping the dead-parent bomb in a conversation. Teddy and I have a long drive ahead of us. And I have the sneaking suspicion he might have a very healthy relationship with two living parents. Hands sweating, I respond as quickly as possible.

"Dead, or, sorry, he's dead. He got sick when I was in high school. Did you ever see the parking lot painted in purple cancer ribbons?"

His head swivels toward me, making brief but direct eye contact before returning his gaze to the road. "I'm so sorry, Marin." He says it slowly and intentionally, with the kind of weight I don't normally get in response to this disclosure. It lands somewhere soft. And I suddenly feel safe. "Of course I saw them. I was doing driver's ed there when they went up and kept wondering who the local celebrity was."

"That was my dad. Wait, was Mr. Lichen your driver's ed teacher?"

At this, Teddy throws back his head, laughing with his whole body, and reaches across the space between us, resting his hand on the headrest of my seat. I expect to tense at the proximity, but there's something settling about his presence there. Mr. Lichen was an instructor that rich parents hired on the side to offer a not-totally-state-sanctioned course condensed into three weeks.

"I had to spend the summer campaigning for student council," he offers. "What was your excuse?" I smile, wondering why it took us eighty miles to break the ice.

"Dead dad." I shrug. "He was about to go into hospice, and my mom needed someone else to cart my sister around as soon as possible." Teddy listens, eyes on the road, his hand still centimeters from my shoulder.

"I can't imagine," he whispers with a reverence I find refreshing from someone I wrote off as unserious. "He'd be proud of you, I'm sure."

I nod, wordless in the way thinking about my dad often makes me. "We don't have to keep talking about it. But thank you."

He moves his hand to the back of my seat to change lanes and then to the wheel. "So you must know my ex, then." Teddy's buzzing—clearly the kind of person powered by nostalgia, who loves a round of regional six degrees of separation. "She's the one who made the 'Sacred Heart Girls Get On Their Knees' T-shirts for our state semifinals against you guys in 2010."

EXIT LANE

I guffaw in response, then quickly gather myself. Should I tell him? I don't have to. I shift in my seat, and I can't quite get comfortable—we're careening toward unbridled honesty, and it feels awkward or maybe unfair to retreat now. The sun is setting, we're three hours in, and it's not like I'll ever see this guy again. I suck in a deep breath as a mischievous smile spreads over my mouth.

TEDDY

My mouth falls open, but I close it again and shake my head firmly. Being next to Marin makes me feel like I'm on my second espresso—nervous, excited, and without a clue as to where things will end up. "No, Maddie's straight."

The suggestion—well, the claim—is that Marin and Maddie hooked up in the back of Marin's Jetta after a homecoming game. I mean, Maddie and I weren't a perfect match, but . . . I watch Marin's face for clues and try not to calculate how much she's drifted toward the center console, unsure whether it's mere observation or wishful thinking.

"No, no. She's a full-send lesbian." Marin can barely get the words out between laughing. Her smile cracks open, and *fuck*. My palms go sweaty, and I drop one hand out the window just to try to dry it off.

Marin folds a leg under her and angles her body toward me. "She went to Smith. Teddy, she had a mullet in *high school*." We laugh—her with abandon, me with nervous realization.

15

"Well, thanks for putting a nail in the coffin of any dream I ever had of marrying my high school sweetheart."

Marin scrunches her nose, like I've said something distasteful. No, I did not think Maddie and I might end up together at this point, but I always liked the idea that maybe I'd have a young-love story like my parents. The picture-perfect marriage that my dad almost ruined when he cheated with his secretary, Carter's aunt, during my junior year of high school. But we're Midwestern. We cried on the sofa and swept it under the rug, and things have been fine ever since. Not that I'm going to mention it to Marin.

"Ok, my turn," I say, changing the subject. "What I know about you is that your best friend is the smartest, most interesting woman at the University of Iowa."

A cop siren sounds to our left. Marin rolls her eyes and manages to explicitly direct this gesture at me. "In this case, Teddy, she's not gay, but it's just never going to happen." It's not really news to me, but I sulk a little anyway.

Marin dismisses my sullen expression with a flick of her wrist, and it feels almost like we're bantering. "Here's what *is* going to happen: Sloane's going to write an Oscar-winning movie, and then we'll go on a thirty-day trip to Japan and renovate brownstones across the street from each other in Brooklyn." It's funny to hear her talk like this. To witness her so excited about a future that's not all that distinct from the one Carter and I picture—just different settings, different trappings. Marin's glowing in the passenger seat, like she's trying to suppress the sunniness Sloane brings out in her but can't.

EXIT LANE

"It sounds like I might not be the only one in love with Sloane Bachman."

Another eye roll. "I'm sure you're too lost in the mire of masculinity to understand a concept like a best friend, but she's mine. So in that sense, she's the love of my life, but I'm not trying to marry her. Or sleep with her, for that matter."

"'The mire of masculinity'?" I crack back. "I'll have you know that my best friend Carter is the love of my life too. And I'm not trying to sleep with him either."

She reaches for her bag of snacks, smirking. "I like that you think you had to tell me you're straight."

I go silent, unsure if I have an opening to ask the question that's been rattling around since she slid into my car: Is Marin only into girls? She's wearing patent loafers and ribbed socks for a cross-country road trip, which feels like it might be my answer, but I don't want to come across as *offensively* straight. And besides, this is just a curiosity triggered by forced proximity and a lack of soundtrack, nothing more. Maybe I just need to leave it alone.

"Tell me a Sloane story," I say instead, navigating past a sputtering semi.

Marin recounts the time Sloane attempted to learn "Edelweiss" on a harp she found at the Iowa City Goodwill the week before a talent show, and I get a chance to take her in. The way she speaks, with her whole body, it's like the words are electricity running through her fingertips. The Diane Keaton comparison was rash. She's languid and boyish, but as I glance over my shoulder to change lanes, I notice a black lace bra beneath her barely buttoned striped oxford. Her hair,

17

a nothing color between brown and blond, seemed unremark-able at first, but the way it falls, framing her face, only for her to push it behind her ears when she's about to make the punch line, delights me.

"And that was when I knew I would grow old with her." Exhausted, she leans back into her seat, doing the hair-behind-her-ears thing again.

"How romantic." I laugh, noticing a sign for a motel in four miles. I hadn't wanted to interrupt her to make a plan, but the piecey sunset has given way to darkness. We have to sleep somewhere.

III

MARIN

The warm air is getting to me. Or maybe it's the darkness. There's an explanation for the sudden urge I feel to share with Teddy all sorts of things I usually don't or won't—I'm just not sure what it is. My usual instinct, especially with new people, is to say less, knowing that control comes from restraint. But I feel an impulse, one generally reserved for flirtation, to see what happens if I give him a little more.

"Maybe Sloane and Carter are the best parts of Iowa, and now that we have them, we'll never have to come back again."

I smooth my pant leg and try not to make it obvious that I'm watching for how he responds. He's less rigid now than he was when we merged onto the interstate four hours ago. His perfect posture has relaxed a little, and the lack of music feels less glaring, by some miracle. I feel tender toward him, which is unnerving—tender is not a feeling I experience, except toward my sister and Sloane. This near stranger has unexpectedly and abruptly transitioned from being someone I planned to ditch as soon as we crossed into Manhattan to one of the few people I'll know there.

Exit signs for Chicago and our first patches of traffic make me wonder when we'll pull over for the night, but I realize I'm not actually ready for our back-and-forth to end.

"'Never have to come back' seems extreme," Teddy starts, curious and compassionate at once. "Can I ask why? Why do you want that? And if it's too much to share with your chauffeur, I get it."

My usual instinct would be to slam the conversational door and get to our destination having exposed as little of myself as possible. But something prods, telling me that it's safe to share, that this is the kind of person who can carry the grief and the sadness, even for a few minutes on the interstate. I don't think twice.

"There's nothing left for me there. After my dad died, it was all people saw when they looked at me—at us. So I'm going to get my sister out, too, when it's time. Then we'll get to be more than kids without a parent. She deserves the space to be more than that."

"Marin, so do you, obviously. That's so much pressure." He glances down before looking at me, and his eyes look watery. "I said this before, but . . ." He tugs on his earlobe a little hard. "Your dad would be proud of you. Any dad would be. You've done a lot, and you're only at the beginning."

My breath catches. This was not my idea of Teddy or my idea of this road trip. Conversations about my dad usually feel like something to power through. My role is to say "I'm OK, I'm OK, I'm OK" or to answer the dreaded "What happened?" questions from people too fixated on their own potential future pain to grasp mine.

Teddy's ability to just sit with it and with me is not a level of empathy I'm accustomed to.

"Well, also, I have a hard time believing I'm going to find a great love story in Iowa," I say, surprising myself. *A great love story? Am I even looking for that?* "Which makes another strong case for getting out into the world." The comment lands somewhere between us, like a challenge or an omen. Teddy stares straight ahead. His jaw opens, closes, and opens again. I try to ignore the way his sunglasses dangle from the bright-white placket of his shirt and tug down the neck. My cheeks warm, and I consciously break the spell, forcing out a laugh before he can respond. "And there's a good chance that, at the very least, the lay of my life is in New York, right?"

TEDDY

I notice her short, neat nails; how her watch rolls on her wrist; and the way she lands her pointer finger on her lip in conversation without thinking. My eyes on the road, I grin every time I make her laugh, and I wonder what other objectives I had before I knew I could get my fix just from seeing her light up.

I am so fixated on memorizing what I can see from my peripheral vision that I almost don't hear her when she instructs me to take the next exit into Joliet. I sit up straighter, check my mirrors, and remind myself that this is a rideshare, a favor to a woman who I've pined after for years.

I pull off the road as Marin directs me and take a deep breath as she climbs out of the car. Unfurling into a stretch, she reaches for the starry sky, revealing a sliver of stomach under her button-down. The parking lot lights catch her skin, and the sign for Envy's Pub feels like it's trying to tell me something. I take another long inhale and open my door.

Walking in together, I'm struck by our almost identical heights, and that I can be differently close to her now that there's not a twelve-inch center console between us. It's 9 p.m. at a sticky dive four minutes off the highway with tater tots and chicken fingers on the menu. "We could have gone somewhere with, uh, a little less character," I offer, clocking a man with an eye patch in the corner throwing darts with impressive accuracy.

"This is on-theme, Teddy," Marin says, lighting a cigarette indoors, which feels apropos. Outside of the Buick, I can take her in the way I might at Donnelly's. Marin's not like any other twenty-two-year-old I've encountered. When she orders us Jamesons on the rocks, I note the certainty in her voice. There's no inflection at the end that makes it sound like a question. There are no filler words. She knows what she wants, and that crystallizes what I want, too. Pushing the sleeves of her blazer up, she spins on her stool to face me—that sliver of a black lace bra peeking through, her legs open in my direction before she crosses them. Every move she makes enhances my regret that we spent the past four years on the same campus but never together.

"Tell me about your watch."

She looks down, spinning the blue-faced Rolex. "It was

EXIT LANE

my dad's. After he died, I started wearing it around the house. Not exactly a popular look for a teen girl. But when I left for Iowa, I started wearing it every day." She pauses and sips her drink. "I don't usually talk about him so much. I'm sorry."

"I like when you talk about him," I say. I reach for a bar napkin and clear my throat. "My dad cheated on my mom in high school." It comes out before I have a chance to consider that I've never told anyone that before. Carter knows—obviously, given the circumstances. We've talked around it. But I've never actually said that sentence aloud.

She winces. "And they stayed together? Your parents?"

I nod and fold the napkin on the diagonal, once, then twice.

She reaches for a napkin of her own. "Everyone has their shit."

I take in Marin's unfixed gaze, and the space between our barstools suddenly feels like a canyon. "Careful." I pull my seat closer to hers so our legs have no choice but to touch. "You might not know me as well as you think you do, boss."

We clink glasses as a plate of onion rings and an entire bottle of Ranch dressing land in front of us.

"Here's to finding out." Marin takes another sip, her eyes never leaving mine.

For an excruciatingly long moment, I don't know what to say, what to do. I'm saved by Marin rolling her eyes. "Oh god," she says. "This song."

"'Hotel California'? What's wrong with it?"

"Please, Teddy. It has to be the least sexy song in the American songbook."

I jump off my stool and dig in my pocket for change. "Is that so?" I grin at her and head for the jukebox, actively ignoring the hundreds of ways I'm picturing this night ending, hoping instead to allow it to unfold as it will.

I play it six times. Every time, she boos, and the leather-skinned motorcyclists on the other end of the bar cheer. We're two, maybe three whiskeys in, and it's a little past eleven.

Marin's flush is back. Our stools are closer, and her gestures are more animated. She laughs into my shoulder, doing the thing where she pushes her hair back, and now it is making my stomach drop in a way that reaches all the way to my dick. Emilie gave me an objectively hot sexual send-off this morning, and here I am losing my bearings over Marin's collarbones, tracing my eyes across her shoulders, shuddering at the thought of compressing the space between us.

"Loose opinions strongly held," she says, dropping two waters in front of us after chatting up a group of truckers near the pitcher at the end of the bar. I shake my head for her to go on. "It's this game Sloane and I always play when we go out. Tell me something inconsequential or abstract you believe in one hundred percent." She taps my chest for emphasis on every syllable of "One. Hun. Dred. Per. Cent." I want to grab her hands, turn them over in my own, and bring them to my lips. Instead, I'm a good sport, though it's becoming harder to determine what that means when it comes to the two of us.

I lean back on my stool, never at a loss for opinions. "Breakups should never happen in person." Marin feigns confusion, leaning her elbow against the bar. She gets this look in her eyes right before she's about to say something cutting. It scares me shitless and also turns me on.

"Ok, that's a strong start. I want to ask why, but I get the vague sense that childhood trauma or a secretly gay high school sweetheart might be to blame."

I laugh. "Your turn."

"Being able to pull off bangs is genetic. Some people are born with it. I am not." Having a younger sister has taught me to never weigh in on the loaded topic of bangs. I nod respectfully and try framing her forehead with the front pieces of her hair. "It kind of works, unfortunately." She's laughing, and I'm a few inches from her face. I wish I could smell her. I wish we were in a place where the scents of fry grease and booze weren't drowning everything else out.

We go back and forth, draining our whiskeys, trading the bartender our bills for quarters so we can keep tormenting each other with the jukebox. Now it's Marin's turn again, and our stools are basically conjoined, and her knee is between my legs.

"You can't get mad at this one. Teddy, please don't take it personally." She holds my shoulders, facing me straight on, her mouth a few inches from mine once again. "Men," her mouth opens slowly in an attempt to prevent a smile, "and women," she's suddenly serious and I get the sick feeling she might not be joking, "can't be friends."

"No, no, no. Objection. Absolutely not. This is surprisingly old-fashioned for a woman like you, Marin."

"I mean it. Take it from someone who's tried friends to lovers and lovers to friends: It's impossible. That's why I have zero male friends." *I guess this answers my question.* The blue of her eyes was a fact in the car, but here in the pub, it's a challenge.

"We're friends." I sigh, taking her hands from my shoulders and holding them in my own. These are sparks—undeniable, storybook sparks—but I mutter, "This is friendship."

She pulls closer, palms on my knees now, close enough for me to smell the smoky perfume on her neck. Close enough to know I'm standing at the cliff of pre-Marin and post-Marin. It's not too early to say this woman could ruin my life. And I'm pretty certain that's exactly what I'm hoping for. "Prove it," she whispers.

I swallow, eyes drifting from the blue of her irises to the muted red of her lips. "I'm going to kiss you right now, and it's not going to change anything," I whisper back, leaving any rational thought behind as I lean in, my mouth grazing hers tentatively, politely. The second the contact registers, everything around us goes blurry. The gleam of the Old Style clock disappears, and the sound of the patrons playing pool mutes. Her hand moves to the soft spot behind my ear, and my heartbeat is in my throat. Her tongue teases mine, and I am instantly hard. I stand, releasing some of the tension in my jeans, and hover over her as I grab the fabric of her button-up in my fist. This is not the feeling of making out with someone at a bar, drunk and desperate. This is

EXIT LANE

hard-earned, the kind of kiss that's trying to say what a thousand words cannot.

Someone cheers from the trucker side of the room. We pull apart.

"Game on," she says, flushed with an impossible lightness in her eyes. "Just friends." She slips off her seat, and I wonder for a second if she's going to lean in and press her lips against mine again. But she turns toward the bathroom.

I smooth my pants, confused, dizzy, and enchanted all at once. Tomorrow we'll be in New York. Tonight I'll think about the words "just friends" coming from Marin's mouth and imagine what else those lips are capable of.

IV

MARIN

I climb into bed at the Best Inn and Suites across the street from the pub. I am actively trying to stop fixating on images of Teddy. His deep-green eyes. They never left me from the second we parked to the moment we started to kiss. The movie projector in my head keeps rolling on the way his pupils dilated as he leaned in with parted lips and pressed them against mine. How he rocked on his back foot, pretending to pick any song other than "Hotel California" at the jukebox, trying not to smile. His jawline. I try tirelessly to think of anything else—this morning with Georgie, my first camp counselor, Tom Selleck in the eighties—but Teddy's the only thing on my brain. I toss and turn on the worn mattress, weighing whether the vibrator somewhere in my bag will help conjure sleep or delay it further. The reality of the situation sinks in the same way it does when I'm fighting a cold or a UTI and attempting to convince myself it's not *really* happening: I have a crush. It is undeniable. I sigh as I pull the scratchy comforter over my head.

EXIT LANE

When I wake up, the sun illuminates the dust in a hotel room that seemed much nicer at midnight after four whiskeys. I turn off my alarm, ignoring a text from Sloane asking how it's going. The question's a little too nuanced for pre-coffee Marin. Today's a Levi's 505 day, plus a massive button-down I rescued from a Salvation Army and the loafers that remind me of where I'm headed—my new life. Despite a laughable attempt at a four-minute meditation, all I can conjure as I pack up my toiletries is the kiss—over and over on a loop. I'd barely had time to imagine what Teddy's mouth would feel like. His gentleness surprised me. It wasn't shyness. It was restraint. A kiss that revealed he'd thought about a lot more than making out at the bar. My hips hollow out at the memory, but I ignore the feeling and sling my duffle over my shoulder. Today's the day I move to New York and leave everything, including last night, behind. *Imagine going to New York and fucking an Iowa boy.*

Pulling the door shut, my emotions a jumble of live wires, I roll my shoulders back, determined to play it as cool as possible. I'm about to start the rest of my life. That's overwhelming enough. As the elevator descends, I find myself attempting to organize my feelings into tidy compartments in my mind and tuck them away. One box for my grief. Another for my anxiety about being so far from Sloane. A third for this sudden tug toward Teddy.

Now he's within my line of sight, standing in the lobby by the coffee station, freshly showered. "Hi," I mutter, trying to avoid eye contact. He looks up, sincere, and gestures as I approach.

"Milk? Or these weird flavored creamers? How'd you sleep?"

"Black," I respond. *I slept like my whole body knew you were just down the hall.*

"Of course." He passes me a cup and reaches for my bag without making it a thing, and we head to the car, me trailing a few steps behind.

The fact of the matter, the ten-hour fact of the matter ahead of us, lingers. Last night happened. But I don't want to talk about it. I buckle myself in and pull on my sunglasses. "Chicago traffic is going to be awful. I'll help navigate."

Indiana's out the windows. Suburban sprawl and cornfields alternate under billboards advertising lawyers and salvation. I glance at Teddy as I snack on pistachios. He's tough to read. Almost like he's been media trained, but it could just be emotional repression—or maybe that's me projecting. His Wayfarers fit his face like a presidential hopeful. I notice his arms—*how many times can I notice his arms?*—muscular under a white T-shirt, and the way his grip is loose but steady on the wheel. His hands make my stomach flip. *Imagining them tracing my body is fair play*, I tell myself. *The second we get to the city, it's over.*

"I still think we'll be friends, Marin," he says, almost at a whisper.

I drop a shelled pistachio into his open palm as a peace offering. He couldn't even wait an hour to bring it up. "I know you do. And I hope we are, Teddy. Someday, maybe you'll be my old friend from Iowa, a place I haven't been in years."

"But why New York?"

I look up and see that we're approaching Cleveland, and the midday sun is hitting Teddy's hair, bringing out the copper tones. I'd been in my own world, at that moment in the kiss loop where he reached his left hand to the small of my waist and tugged on my belt loop. Daydreaming about a person in his presence is a universal sign you're a goner. So is sharing vulnerable childhood memories.

"My dad took me to New York when I was eleven. Just me and him—not my sister, not my mom. He said I was his city kid. We saw Broadway shows and ate nachos at a fancy restaurant in Central Park."

"Nachos at a fancy restaurant sounds like a perfect date, honestly."

I laugh, trying not to linger on the choice of the word "date" and continue. Teddy keeps messing with the nonexistent AC and finding reasons for his hand to drift across the imagined boundary between us.

"New York was a completely different world. And even then, as a kid, I fell in love with that idea. I knew I'd come back, and then when he died, it was the thing I latched on to. This notion that life could and would be different in almost every way. I could and would be different if I could just get to the city."

We're quiet, and I think about the magnetic pull New York has had on me for almost half my life. Starting over there is all I ever hope for. Though I sometimes question what it says about me that my future looks like a place, I've been grateful to have a destination to cling to, even if the rest of my vision lacks . . . vision. Even though we just met, Teddy is part of my old life, the past I'm desperate to shed. And as daunted as I am to start from scratch, I can't have someone I met a day ago hold me back.

Teddy looks over, worried. I wonder if he assumes my silence has to do with nerves, or the way his hand had wrapped around my neck like an old habit when we kissed, or the things we've divulged to each other already. It's somehow all of that and none of that.

"Well, I've never been, and I'm terrified."

I pause before responding, considering whether I find this relatable. I am terrified, but I'm not scared of the city. What I fear is anything that might pull me away from it. "You'll have new classmates and built-in structure," I say, and he nods like he needs to hear it. "You'll do great." I rest my head on the window.

He stretches out his right arm, and I hold my breath, wondering if he's going to touch my shoulder. But instead he reaches behind us and grabs one of his pillows from the Tetris of the back row—books, garbage bags of sweaters. "Try getting some rest," he says as he tucks it between me and the headrest.

EXIT LANE

TEDDY

Marin is asleep practically on my lap, and I'm having a hard time parceling my nerves for law school and my inability to pinpoint my feelings about her. That's what I-80 East is good for, I guess. Last night was a fluke—not indiscretion but a perfect storm of whiskey, nervous excitement, and a small-town cast of supporting characters. This explanation does not account for the fact that within minutes of safety-locking the door of my hotel room, I was coming into my hand. So much pent-up desire that all it took was a few strokes, and I was done, like I was sixteen again. I organize all my thoughts on a mental whiteboard while she naps, careful to stick within five miles of the speed limit. I'll graduate from NYU. Get a job at a top law firm after impressive summer internships and perfect grades. Make lifelong friends and avoid alcoholism. Meet the woman I'm destined to marry—at a mutual friend's birthday, maybe, and who would guess that she's also ready to move back to the Midwest? Buy the house next to Carter's grandma's on Fifty-First Street. Pass the Iowa bar. Forget about this road trip in a matter of two to seven years.

My dad risked the balance of our life when he cheated, and it didn't take more than three therapy sessions for me to realize that every decision I make is an attempt to conjure compulsory stability. Wanting things to be settled and safe is how I cope. I just wonder how Marin, potentially the total antithesis to my plan, fits.

We're closer now, and the GPS countdown haunts me

from where my phone is propped against the ashtray mount. The inevitability of this drive ending makes my stomach turn, my brain desperately scrambling to make sense of my feelings for Marin before our arrival.

I'm starving, I realize. The last proper meal we ate were those onion rings for dinner. Carefully, I pull over to search for sandwiches nearby. I don't want to wake Marin. I get the sense she doesn't allow herself to rest like this very often. Her forehead softens. There's a piece of hair I want to push behind her ear.

As I pull up to a sub shop, I text Sloane to find out Marin's ideal sandwich order. She responds immediately. "She wants an Italian Night Club, but if you ask, she'll say she wants a Tuna Club." Italian it is. It doesn't occur to me until I'm contemplating the chip selection at checkout that my exchange with Sloane wasn't tinged with the same fraught thrill I usually experience with any interaction with her.

I wait to eat until Marin wakes up, twenty minutes later. Unwrapping our sandwiches together in the late afternoon light strikes me as somehow romantically charged. So mundane as to be intimate. A distinctly different experience than I've had consuming dozens of other Turkey Toms in my life. I stuff that notion somewhere unseen.

"Salt and vinegar. Bold choice," she says, opening the chips I got us to share. "I respect it."

We reach at the same time, hands brushing, and I promise myself she didn't feel what I just felt. Except she's blushing.

EXIT LANE

It would be simpler to kiss her, but I scan my brain for conversation topics instead, trying to toe the line between making it obvious I want to know everything about her and keeping things chatty. Before I come up with anything, she asks, "What are you most nervous about?" She licks chip dust off a finger and twists her hair into a bun.

You, I want to say. I tug my ear until it hurts just enough to focus me. "Being away from Carter and my family," I offer instead. "And about school. And the subway. Rats, too. I'm sure there were rats in the Midwest, but I didn't see them. What if my MetroCard doesn't work or I ask for Ranch and someone makes fun of me? I'm nervous about a lot." It's all out before I have the chance to self-edit.

Marin nods. *She's the coolest person I've ever met*, I think. Both in presentation and in demeanor. It's like her emotions are buried beneath layers of steel. I've never once known what she's thinking in the twenty-four hours we've been together except for when we were kissing. Even her body language, the way she rolls her neck and fixes her gaze out the window, makes me feel like she's a thousand miles away.

Until she responds in a quiet voice, "I'm nervous about everything, too."

Before I can reply, the Buick hits a pothole, and the cassette tape player, defunct for years, slams into place. Kenny Loggins's "Danger Zone" starts playing.

Marin laughs, and once she gets going, she can't stop. She grips the dash, and her smile is the brightest I've seen. I'd do anything to see more of it, so I start singing, and I do

35

a pretty impressive Loggins impression. It's like this cracks the code of her emotional safe, and she lets go. She lets me see her. She joins in before the chorus swells, and soon we're both at top volume with the windows hand-cranked open on the interstate. At the last verse, I turn to notice she's tearing up. "Eyes on the road," she mutters, pulling her sunglasses down from where she perched them on top of her head and shoving my shoulder. But it's too late. Now I'm crying and not even trying to hide it, thinking about speeding into the unknown and wanting everything I left behind to stay the same in my absence.

It's us, a few semitrucks, and the raucous chorus over the speakers. It's funny how music really does make the drive go faster. Marin's hair has come loose, and she's using her hair clip as a microphone. I've opted for steering-wheel drums, and we're both out of breath by the time the song ends.

"I promise to never bring up the time we both cried to Kenny Loggins in your dead grandma's Buick," Marin says, her face soft and kind before her eyes narrow. I can tell she doesn't want to say whatever's next. "I'm thinking we can sort of pretend like this entire road trip never happened if that's OK with you."

My stomach, a whirlpool of nerves and excitement, drops. Rationally, I'm aligned. But what happened last night—the twenty-second clip of Marin pulling me in, slipping her tongue into my mouth, tracing it across my own before pulling away—has been the only concrete fact I can trust. I thought we'd laugh about it over beers, maybe drive back to Iowa for a holiday, or see a movie on a Tuesday

EXIT LANE

night some time. But the pit in my stomach, the sucker punch of her announcement, has me rethinking everything.

"You got it, boss. Never happened." I'm stuck behind every other vehicle trying to enter the Holland Tunnel, and suddenly the minutes I have left with this car, this cassette tape, and this girl I met yesterday can't pass quickly enough.

MARIN

"Good luck with everything." I'm standing next to a small pile of suitcases, milk crates, and the odd art object on the curb of Eighty-Third Street. My cousin's room awaits me five flights up. A thousand beats per minute feels accurate for my current heart rate. Strangers file past us, ignoring what must be an everyday occurrence to them. I don't want to hurt his feelings, but I think it might be too late for that. If my proposal to mind wipe the road trip didn't do it, my refusal to let him help me carry my stuff inside certainly did. I remind myself to stay focused on what's in front of me, mentally silencing the kiss, the sandwich order—the Kenny fucking Loggins of it all.

Teddy's shifting from one foot to the other on the curb, barely making eye contact. The sad-puppy energy is working on me more than I'll ever let on. But I know if we keep up this shoddy attempt at friendship, things will only get murkier. "That sounded harsh. I mean, have a good life." I shake my head. "Ok, well, that's worse." I can't make sense of how to say goodbye to someone I can't stop thinking about but who I hope I never see again. It comes down to this: I need a fresh start more than I need Teddy.

He's just out of grasp from where I'm leaning against the front gate. We're silent for a full minute, his eyes reaching for mine, which I fix on a lamppost across the street. "Why can't it just be 'see you soon'?" His voice is low but clear. A little pleading.

The question tugs at some small part of me, threatening to undo everything that got me here. He reaches for my hands, which are shaking and sweaty. Dead giveaways of why we can't.

"I—I'm sorry, Teddy. I don't want to disappoint you."

He laughs. "It's New York. We'll be a few miles away. Let's just see, OK? Friends?"

I let him take my palms, and I'm keenly aware of the electricity pulsing between us. "Maybe we're meant to be old friends who lost touch."

THREE YEARS LATER

V

MARIN

"You never make time for yourself." Sloane's lecturing me during my commute home to Tribeca from my office. Most nights, I opt out of the comped Uber to give her a call while I walk the thirty minutes back to my place. Tonight's topic: my inability to let loose. "One night a week where you're not glued to Slack isn't exactly *balance*, Mar. Violet told me you're going into the office on Sundays, too." There are perks to Sloane being nearly as close as I am with my little sister; them teaming up on me isn't one of them.

"I'm fine. I promise I'm fine. It's just temporary. And I'm way better now that I'm with Gabby, I promise." Even with the sounds of traffic, I can hear her sigh.

"I know you think that—and I'm glad you do—but you'll make yourself sick if you keep this up. Come back to Iowa for Violet's show choir showcase. We all miss you."

Something catches in my throat, and I ignore it, barreling through a crosswalk beneath a blinking hand. "I know, and I really want to, but this deal is important. I'll be home for Christmas."

I've been working at FourVC since my internship, and

now I specialize in consumer research. Which is like being paid for the shit talking Sloane and I used to do after Mug Night at Donnelly's. "No one wants to smoke cigarettes anymore. When did Gatorade make a comeback? If I see one more med spa pop up in an empty bank . . ." That sort of thing. They put a full-time offer in front of me right after the fitness start-up I'd convinced them to back sold to a giant athleisure conglomerate less than a year after they'd invested in their Series B. That this sort of thing comes naturally to me is both a blessing and a curse: I'm on the fast track to becoming a partner at the firm, but everything else in my life is in the slow lane.

Sloane lets it go, asks when she'll meet my mysterious quasi girlfriend, and signs off with our signature "See you soon," even though it's been almost a year since we've been in the same room.

I fire Gabby a text, suggesting takeout at mine, despite it being well before the commonly acknowledged booty call hour of 9 p.m. I like spending time with Gabby, and I do it a few days a week, but I'm not sure I'm committed to *her* so much as to the simplicity of our dynamic. Engaging in something serious feels impossible right now, but I like her and have yet to tire of her after a few months in. There's no running back our sex like a movie scene in my head, sure, but it's comfortingly uncomplicated—and that's good for now.

"Be there in twenty," she writes back. I hustle the rest of the way home, fluff sofa pillows, and give my apartment as objective a once-over as I can. My job has its cons—

EXIT LANE

namely, that it swallows up all my time and most of my friendships—but it also has its pros, including a salary I didn't know was possible at twenty-five. One that, growing up in Iowa, I assumed only existed in magazines. And one that allows me to order Gabby's favorite sushi any random night without thinking about it.

"This *week*," Gabby says as she walks into my apartment, kisses me, and drops a bottle of chilled red on the counter. She's my age, runs the social team for a presidential hopeful, and has a body that should be immortalized in marble. We met on Raya, and we never talk about life outside of work or when we can see each other next. I barely know anything about her family, and I prefer it that way. I'll share about my dad when it comes up, and it hasn't yet. The last time I told someone new about him was on a highway outside of the state of New York, and I'm happy to keep it that way.

Dressed in a leather jacket and ripped-to-shreds jeans, Gabby pulls a corkscrew out of the drawer by my fridge and leaves it next to the wine. "Here's the plan." Gabby reaches for my wrist and tugs me toward the sofa. She kisses my neck, and with every contact, I feel the tension headache I've been carrying since my second espresso soften. "We'll fuck. We'll drink this wine. We'll eat. And then we're going out." Unzipping her pants and tugging at her shirt, I silence everything but the present moment.

Afterward, it's two quick glasses of Lambrusco, a spread of hand rolls, and a half-assed outfit change as she hustles me out the door. My hair's falling out of a braid, and Gabby

43

laughs as I wrap a huge cashmere sweater over my shoulders and stuff my keys and cards into my pockets. "You're dressed like someone who can't wait to get back home."

Smiling, reminding myself to be here, now, I pull her into me. "Trust me, I can't."

TEDDY

When Carter calls, I'm on my way to Judicial Oversight—my law school cohort's weekly reunion at Josie's on East Sixth Street—and ready to forget about work. My former roommates like to give me shit for not upgrading to a doorman building with a poolroom when we all landed Big Law salaries, but low rent and proximity to dives like the one I'm headed to can't be argued with.

"You won't guess who I've been emailing with," Carter says. I pause. Knowing him, it could be truly anyone. He's still in Nevada, hiking most weekends and FaceTiming me whenever our schedules allow. "Sloane. From undergrad? Your eternal crush?"

Of course I recall, but the eternal feels long expired. I can tell he's waiting for a reaction. "What have you been emailing about?"

"A desert apocalypse short film. She posted about it. I'd seen it—it was shot around here—and reached out."

"Ah, of course. A desert apocalypse short film."

"Her best friend, remember her? The tall one you gave a lift to after graduation? She's still in the city too, apparently."

EXIT LANE

My lips turn up toward a smile, but I force them down. *Remember her? Grave understatement.* Most of the time, though, I wish I didn't. Hearing Carter casually mention a person who's been trapped in my head for so long lands me right in my body. Like she's real again. I feel the pull of my jacket across my shoulders. I tug my ear. I cough.

It's been three years since I dropped her off on the Upper East Side, and I've never been able to forget about Marin Voss for very long. Sometimes, when I'm drunk enough, I still get off thinking about that night outside of Chicago. Nothing happened—or almost nothing happened—but the memory remains crystal clear, ready to be conjured. "Marin," I say, stopping outside of the bar.

"Did you ever see her after the road trip?"

"She was pretty adamant about that drive being the start and end of our friendship." My tone's more defensive than I mean for it to sound. Carter knows me better than anyone, and this is a dead giveaway.

"Ah. It was like that."

"Carter."

"Ok, well, she has some big job now just like you have some big job now. And you're both still there."

"We have so much in common."

"I'm just saying."

"Listen, I gotta go, but next time, you'll tell me more about what you're 'just saying' to Sloane."

He laughs. "See you soon."

My usual crew of former classmates and plus-ones waves

45

from the booth in the corner. After doing close readings of contracts for five hours, I welcome this release with people who've been heads-down on the same type of thing and have zero interest in talking about it.

I give cheek kisses to the women and awkward half hugs to the men. "Anyone need anything?"

Cleo, who I know from my first internship, squeezes my elbow. "When you're back, remind me to tell you about someone else I want to set you up with. If you'll give me a second chance at matchmaking."

"Of course," I say, but my heart isn't in it. It never is. I like meeting new people, but by the third date, it almost always becomes clear there isn't much there. I try to remind myself that it takes time—and that feeling connected to someone doesn't just happen. But I either get too depressed about the prospect of talking about what TV shows we're watching and end it early or accept inertia, let a relationship take hold, and wait to be broken up with a few months later for "being distant."

As I stand at the bar and wait for my beer, I try to shake the malaise that's come over me during the last half hour. *You're here to catch up with friends. Don't get like this.* I grab a black napkin and fold it once, twice. When my eyes scan toward the booth, they snag on the back of a head I'd recognize anywhere. I tell myself it's someone else, that there's no reason she'd be at a linoleum-floored downtown bar playing Merle Haggard. But then she turns to face a beautiful woman in a leather jacket, and I see her T-shirt: "Sacred Heart Girls Get On Their Knees."

VI

MARIN

It's hard to argue with Gabby as I lean into a pool stance with one hand on a whiskey soda and one eye on the cue ball. Josie's is electric. And sticky. And she herself is stunning, backlit by the streetlights outside the window and smiling at me. As I lean in for a kiss, I hear my name. "Marin?"

My instinctual response to that voice: delight. That's before I have time to start a list of a hundred reasons why it can't be him. Because there's no way he stayed in the city after school. I'm sure he moved back to Iowa and has sent out save the dates for a wedding at the Des Moines Botanical Garden in late spring. As my rational brain makes its case, Teddy McCarrel steps in front of me and skims his fingers along the green felt of the table.

It's like I'm seeing him in Technicolor after years of black and white. His posture. The hints of copper in his brown hair. Just the sight of his hands makes me embarrassed to remember all the times I've thought about his tongue brushing against mine while I've touched myself. I might have gotten off at the thought of him as recently

47

as last week. That kiss, the wave goodbye from the curb, all of it lives staunchly in the past tense. When I think about him, about those two days, it's like the memory is encased in a museum—untouchable, protected, and precious. Teddy is a relic to me, and to see him here, in present tense, throws off my balance. I shift from heel to toe in my loafers, and the flutter I feel in my stomach makes me realize it's been three years since I last felt this sensation.

I watch him reach toward me in what we both expect to be a bear hug, but he changes his mind with his arms extended and places his hand on my shoulder. The weight of him there is somehow more intimate than the press of our bodies would have been. It takes me back to the bucket seats, the manual windows, the busted radio, the fears shared. His hair's a little longer, and he seems right at home in New York, something I could have never guessed for the bright-eyed boy who dropped me off uptown. But I'm not the same as I was then either. I've been back to Iowa a few times—weddings, holidays, my grandma's funeral. Every ticket to DSM a step backward and every return flight to JFK a reminder that my real life is here, where I've become the version of myself I dreamed of ever since my dad died. I'm ironclad. I can take care of myself. I don't need more than I have. And now Teddy, appearing in front of me, reminds me of all the ways he makes me feel otherwise.

"Hi, Teddy." I lean my pool stick upright, reaching a hand out to shake his. I'm feigning formality, but really, I want to feel the press of his palm against mine. Gabby watches with amusement.

EXIT LANE

"It's been so long," he says, his eyes tracing the planes of my face. "Or . . . how are you?"

I think about the way we left things—the way I left things—and how as much as I've lingered on my memories of Teddy, it never occurred to me that I would ever see him again. At twenty-two, I was too naive to know that New York could feel like a small town. The sort of place where you run into the guy you have sex dreams about at a bar you've never been to before. But I'm older now, and somehow, I still hadn't thought to imagine this.

"Oh, hi, I'm Teddy." As he reaches out to shake Gabby's hand, I brace for the interaction to reverberate with awkwardness. But I'm not giving Teddy enough credit for what seems to be his spiritual gift: charging through uncomfortable conversations with a disarming smile and the kind of casual confidence that puts him at ease in any social situation. I forgot how attractive it is.

He clears his throat and turns back toward me. "Where in the city are you these days?" It's a safe question, one you can ask a colleague.

"Nearby," I offer, unwilling to give specifics. I was planning on ordering in and getting laid. But here I am cagily introducing my not-quite girlfriend to my not-quite friend.

"Me, too, actually." His eyes spark, like a challenge. "By Washington Square Park. I can't believe we're just now bumping into each other."

"How do you guys know—" Gabby's trying to read us, I realize.

"Iowa, technically. But make no mistake, Marin and I

were not friends. I simply escorted her to the city in my busted, hand-me-down Buick at Sloane's insistence, and then Marin told me she never wanted to see me again."

Is that what I said?

"Sorry, who's Sloane?" Gabby turns to me now, and it hits me. I've never mentioned my best friend to her in the four months we've been quasi together. Gabby doesn't know the most important person in my life's first name.

"Uh, my college roommate, sorry. I'm sure I've brought her up. I haven't seen her in a long time." I try to downplay the relationship to soften the blow, but then I feel like an asshole for acting like Sloane means anything less to me than she does. "She set up—not, like, romantically—she set up me and Teddy to drive here on graduation day."

I try my best to look totally unfazed by the mess I'm making with this run-in and how I'll have to clean it up later.

Teddy's eyes search for mine, and I make an effort to avoid his gaze. The appropriate thing would be to actually introduce Gabby and tell him we're dating, but I can't bring myself to. "Nice catching up with you," I say instead, reaching for my pool cue.

He laughs, like he's genuinely charmed by my dismissiveness. "Is that what we just did? Well, hope to do it again soon."

I tuck a loose strand of hair behind my ear, and he tracks the movement, bites his lip, and turns back toward his group.

Determined to prove to myself and to Gabby that the

EXIT LANE

Teddy run-in was in fact innocuous, I finish the game, grab her hand, and drag her to the musty bathroom.

"Who is that puppy dog of a man, and what did you do to him?" she asks as I slip off her jacket and sling it over the sink.

I laugh, kissing the spot where her neck meets her shoulder, but I'm finding it hard to focus. "Teddy was my long-haul Uber driver. He was obsessed with Sloane." I'm on my knees, pulling at Gabby's jeans, desperate for her, trying not to correlate the sudden need I feel with the man I just saw. I am reckless, untethered. *It was that call with* Sloane *earlier*, I tell myself. It has nothing to do with seeing the ghost of Teddy Past.

"Hey—" She plays with my braid. "Can this wait until we're back at yours?" She's trying to let me down gently. She's seen me hungry but never . . . depraved. Never with all caution and cleanliness abandoned. "Come on," she says, reaching for my elbow. "I'll get you a real drink somewhere with proper lighting."

As we settle into a bar down the street with twenty-dollar cocktails, I take in Gabby. She is the most beautiful person here, easy. And yet, I am angled toward the street, straightening my back at the sight of anyone who looks remotely like Teddy walking by. I refuse to try to determine whether it's something I'm avoiding or all I'm hoping for.

Gabby takes a work call outside, and I join her to smoke. The ancient cigarette at the bottom of my bag's a pretty lame excuse to scan the other side of the street. Her face hardens on the phone, one hand blocking the other ear.

"It's kind of important." She rolls her eyes. "I have to deal with it. But it'll just be a few hours. Finish your drink. I'll meet you back at yours."

I don't know what time it is, but I nod. I kiss the corner of her mouth goodbye.

Living in the city feels like a fact of my life, as natural as the weather. But nursing a Manhattan alone at a bar on a Wednesday night is exactly the type of scenario that reminds me of the wonder and improbability of it all. I pay the tab and walk the sidewalks the same way I used to when I first got here. I try to push Teddy into the recesses of my subconscious in the same way I used to when I first got here. All I've programmed myself to care about is work, my sister, my mom, and Sloane. Realizing I never told Gabby about Sloane, let alone my dad, makes my stomach turn. I can't land on a reasonable explanation. I decide to keep wandering while my feelings crystallize. The farther I inch my way uptown, the clearer my desires become. I might not know exactly what my next move is, but I am sure of one thing: There's only one way to end this night.

TEDDY

Of course the first time I see Marin in three years, she's making out with the second-most beautiful woman in Josie's. My instinct was to run onto the street, call Carter, tell him that not only do I think about Marin every day but that I just saw her, in the flesh, as if his call conjured

EXIT LANE

her. But instead I stayed put, because it meant that I could watch her, even if only out of my peripheral vision, even if it was to see her slip into the bathroom with someone else. She's still Marin. I'm still me.

"You sure you're up for this?" Cleo asks. "You look pale." I nod, pulling on my jacket to follow the rest of our pared-down crew to St. Mark's Place. At some point, Sad Girl Karaoke became the official Judicial Oversight after-party. The one rule: only ballads and singer-songwriters. It makes for horrible performances and the best time. We roll up, nodding at our usual guy who brings pitchers of lukewarm beer into the private room before we can even open the laminated songbook. Someone chooses Bonnie Raitt, our patron saint of SGK. But tonight, even a criminally bad rendition of "Case of You" can't keep my mind from racing. Marin was right there. And I couldn't even get her number or ask her for coffee. And what if I had? It's not like she'd want to be friends. I'm sure she's forgotten about the drive mostly, the kiss entirely.

When it's my turn, I flub what was meant to be a heart-wrenching cover of "Closer to Fine," triggering a round of Miller Lites on me. Three steps from the bar, I stop dead in my tracks at the sight of a sweatered shoulder pulling a whiskey shot. Its owner is bent over the surface, conspiring with the bartender. I see the flash of a smile I memorized years ago. It's a mirage, brought to me by the combination of beer, Indigo Girls, and hyperfixation. I swear I've never felt the divine appointance of luck like this in my life. If it is, in fact, Marin Voss, I promise myself I won't mess it up.

Her presence, even unconfirmed, calms something in

me. I feel like I'm wearing horse blinders, unaware of a world outside of this single frame with her in it. She makes sense of everything in a way that makes no sense, and her mere proximity calls forth the calming hum of the tires on the road that brought us to where we are now. It might be fate or God or the waning number of East Village establishments open at this hour, but it feels like I've won the lottery twice in one night.

She grabs her drink, turns, and sees me. I hold my breath for her reaction—a response unburdened by the knowledge that I'm watching. When she smiles, every muscle in my body goes limp.

"Teddy McCarrel, you're stalking me." The way she says it, laughing and shoving my shoulder as she approaches me, I have to remind myself to breathe.

"Marin Voss, this is my territory. You can have Baby Grand, but Sing Sing is mine." She laughs. We're a barstool away from each other.

I search for her companion from before. "Solo at Wednesday night karaoke? Where's your girlfriend?"

"She had work stuff come up. I wasn't ready to go home yet." I watch her debate elaborating. "Solo karaoke seemed . . . cathartic. And for what it's worth: not quite a girlfriend."

Before I can take it all in—cathartic, not quite a girlfriend—she continues, "Are you here alone, too?"

The idea of explaining Sad Girl Karaoke to Marin or introducing her to my friends makes my languid muscles tense. "My friends are just wrapping up," I fib.

EXIT LANE

Her blue eyes—*how did I forget the intensity of that blue?*—light up. "I have another hour in a private room, and I'm pretty sure karaoke bars lose their license if they don't include 'Hotel California' in their songbook."

And so I sing "the least sexy song in recent American history" to Marin, who leans against a shiny black banquette that lines the dark room. She's cackling, her shirt untucked like the smallest crack in her cool-girl veneer. Any shot I have at sex appeal is ruined by my inability to stay on key.

"Your turn," I say, trading the microphone for the beer we promised to split, our sorry attempt at good decision-making at 3 a.m. on a school night. Our hands touch, and I savor the brush of her fingertips across my knuckles. We both inhale when she jokingly puts her arm around my shoulder. I want to kiss her. Ask her if she misses me the way I miss her. Promise we'll never go years without seeing each other. But instead, I just smile.

"I'm about to perform the ultimate karaoke song." She's speaking into the microphone with feigned seriousness, addressing an imaginary audience. I take it as my cue to sit. I spread my arm across the back of the seat and try to stop imagining pulling her to my lap. "It's my go-to. It's my life's song. And without further ado, Teddy, please select song 2944."

The screen goes black before it flashes purple. "Starfish and Coffee" begins, and I shake my head and smile. Marin's voice is the kind of sound you'd expect from someone who sang in choir since she was seven. She's clear and confident and charming as hell. Her eye contact is unwavering, and it's impossible to deny her magnetism. If I could press pause and stay here, I would. As she rocks her weight to the toes of her loafers, I consider how she dresses. From the day I picked her up in my car, I've interpreted it as a way of signaling to guys like me that she's not looking for approval. And yet I judge the stupid crossbody chain bag and leather leggings of every woman I meet against her improbably sexy worn-in Levi's and blazers. She holds her beer like a John Hughes character. When she thinks no one's watching, she lets her face soften, and it's like she's opening a door to a part of herself no one, except maybe Sloane and her family, knows.

When she finishes with a bow, I stand, hugging her for no reason other than a need to be near her. My heart is racing, and I think I can feel hers doing the same. The smell of her—smoky still, but more herbal, brighter than I remember—grabs ahold of me. "Prince is my religion," she says, collapsing onto the bench, that same black lace bra slipping into view.

"Close your eyes," I instruct, typing in the numbers for my own signature karaoke track, desperate to focus on something other than the image of Marin's body pressed against mine.

I start singing. Two lines in, Marin jumps to her feet, and she's screeching: "This was my sexual awakening!" Now, we're splitting the mic, and she's air-guitaring in the sincerest way through the chorus of "Darling Nikki," followed by every other Prince track Sing Sing has to offer. I accuse Marin of crying during "Nothing Compares 2 U," but she denies it. We both do dramatic body rolls during "Adore"—an effort to ignore the sentiment of the lyrics on my part.

Then it's four in the morning, and it's closing time. I'm tipsy, happy, and tired, and I half expect to see the LeSabre parked outside on St. Mark's Place. Marin lights a cigarette and leans against a wrought-iron gate. If this was a date, I'd ask her back to my apartment. *No*, it dawns on me. *If this was a date, I'd ask her to spend the rest of her life with me.*

I tuck the thought away to interrogate later. "That was very close to friendship, Marin. I rarely karaoke with strangers or enemies."

She takes a drag, shaking her head like it's all a game. "We'll run into each other again." The look on her face tells me she wants to believe this as much as I do. "But this isn't me. I don't stay out this late. I had the best time"—she presses her hands against my chest—"but this wasn't real."

My stomach does a roller-coaster drop. How does she always manage to catch me off balance? Before I can contest, she's hailing a cab, flicking the cigarette, and waving goodbye in one fell swoop.

I stand there, dazed. What just happened? Then, fuck, she's gone again. As I trudge my way to the corner, I'm the guy walking home who can't stop thinking about a girl who'll never want him. I feel unmoored. I reach for my phone to text the last three women I hooked up with until I notice dollar pizza shops locking up. *Don't be sloppy*, I tell myself as I sulk down Lafayette.

Home, I kick off my shoes, tug off my pants, and climb

into bed, ignoring every bodily urge to drink water or at least take a shower. Staring at the spot where the ceiling burst open during a rainstorm last year, I think about Marin, and my dick grows hard at the image of her leaning against the banquette, one heel out of her shoe, her mouth half open in delight. I jerk off, imagining what it would have been like if I'd leaned in to kiss her outside Sing Sing. The fantasy is a far cry from what it usually takes to get me there. I roll over onto my side and press my face into my pillow. *Maybe this will be like an exorcism*, I think. Now I'll try to forget her. I close my eyes and sigh. Right—since that worked so well last time.

MARIN

Driving across town, I stick my head out the window of the taxi, bartering with the fresh air to give my brain oxygen and bring me back to my real life and the very real person waiting for me at my apartment, hopefully asleep by now. How do I spin this? A bunch of us went to karaoke at the last minute. Teddy kept buying rounds. No, no mention of Teddy. Before I have the chance to land on a concrete narrative, I'm stepping out onto the block I still can't believe is mine. I didn't build this life in New York by fucking around with a random guy I met one time in Iowa.

Singing with him reminded me of our Kenny Loggins rendition but also of those nights out with Sloane when we kept finding reasons not to go home. I could have sat

EXIT LANE

talking to him on a curb for hours, watching the sunrise over the East River. Being with Teddy is easy—when I don't get so wrapped up in micromanaging my feelings that it's confusing and terrifying.

I give myself the moment between pressing the button for the elevator and its actual arrival to picture a world where all that means something: one where it's me and Teddy. Where I let him know me and see me. Where I uncork the feelings I keep bottled up. Where I'm a totally different person.

But on the ride to my floor, I make a list of all the reasons why it doesn't mean anything. We were drunk. It was a matter of chance that I ran into him, twice. I'd sing my favorite Prince song in a private karaoke room with anyone. None of my arguments are strong enough to stand on their own, so I land on this: Teddy isn't part of my new life. It's as simple as that.

I open my front door to Gabby at the dining room table, and the glare she gives me almost sends me back into the hallway. "Hey. I can't believe you're still working." I walk behind her and massage her shoulders, which feel tighter than usual. There's a sea of notes spread around her.

She turns her head to look up at me, like she's seeing me for the first time. "I can't believe you're just getting home. I've known you for four months, and you've never stayed up past midnight. Where were you?" Her tone isn't accusatory; it's perplexed.

"Karaoke?"

"You, Marin, did karaoke? Is this a joke? I've never

59

even heard you hum. When I tried to get you to go to Metropolitan, you told me, and I quote, 'Karaoke is for unserious people.'"

"That was group karaoke. This was a private room, much different. Babe, it's just karaoke. I'm home now."

There's a look on Gabby's face—tight jaw and raised eyebrows—that makes me realize she has something to say. Every inch of me wants to lock myself in the bathroom and cover my ears. I am woefully unprepared for a confrontation right now. She folds her arms as I walk over to sit across from her at the table, finally willing to admit I have zero idea where this night will end.

"You never stay out late with me. I didn't even know you sing. I don't recognize you like this." She sighs, pulling her papers into a pile. "You've never mentioned Sloane. I've met zero of your friends. Marin, I don't even know if you have friends." She pauses, reloading, and I lean back to take it—apprehensive of the calm I feel coursing through my veins. "I wanted this . . . whatever this is, to work. You're brilliant and so hot and ambitious in a way that appeals to me, but you're not ready for something real," she whispers, pulling my hand into her chest. "And I think there's so much that has to happen before you are."

My guard's up as she grabs her skincare from the shower and requests a car before giving me a kiss goodbye on the cheek. "Call me in a few years. And maybe call that boy from the bar. I've never seen you light up like that."

When she walks out, I want to collapse onto my bed, meditate for a while, and maybe FaceTime Sloane. But

EXIT LANE

instead, I grab my phone and check my work email. There, I can lose myself in the calls and decks and itineraries for last-minute flights to SFO. There, I can try to escape the image of Teddy, his head thrown back and his hand gripping the microphone like it was his life-force, belting out a song about being there until the end of time.

TWO YEARS LATER

VII

TEDDY

I try to be subtle as I crane my neck up at the imposing Union Square office building, but I let myself linger long enough to be anything but. Maybe taking stock right now will help settle me. It's my first day at FourVC, a company my dad keeps referring to as ThreeVC. The whole thing happened fast. They needed in-house counsel. A recruiter reached out, and soon I had an offer. Cue me on the phone with Carter: "I never thought I'd make even half of this salary at any point in my life, Cart."

"I love this news." There's a long pause, long enough to make me question if our connection dropped. "Not to make it weird, but isn't that where Marin works?" His relationship with Sloane had transitioned from epistolary into a full-fledged long-distance romance. Which means he knows the contours of Marin's life—and probably more—though we avoid acknowledging that most of the time.

"It's a big company. And I'm sure she'll be too busy yelling at an intern from her corner office to even notice." I try to play it like I haven't done thorough LinkedIn stalking, hadn't thought about reaching out to her when I got the job. But given how many years we've technically known each

65

other—five—and how many interactions we've technically had—two—I decided to respect that she doesn't want to hear from me. She's made it abundantly clear. I'll be the droning lawyer reminding her annually about statutory best practices via company-wide emails she probably won't even open.

Sitting in the impeccably sterile lobby, I bury my Marin nerves under my new-job nerves until a friendly receptionist guides me to my desk. The views from the window I face are impressive, but not enough to stop me from scanning the office for her. I hope my curiosity reads as if I'm actively taking in my new surroundings, and I hope the disappointment I feel at her apparent absence doesn't show. People start clearing out around six, and I finally work up the nerve to ask about her. *Just to know*, I tell myself as I approach the receptionist typing away at his desktop. It's strange—creepy, even—not to say hi.

"Hey, Jesse, right? So I wonder if, um . . . Marin Voss works here, right?"

Jesse smiles, his eyes never leaving the computer screen.

"She relocated to Copenhagen last year to be closer to a couple of her portfolio companies. Was it last year? Had to have been. But she's back in the office all the time. Want me to see if I can put a virtual coffee on her calendar?"

"No, no, but thanks, Jesse." Defeated, and maybe a little relieved, I pack my bag and mentally catalog my to-dos for the evening. Call back my dad's doctor, the one he saw when he dealt with a bout of skin cancer a few years ago, and get a referral. Respond to a text from Caroline, my girlfriend of eight months, to confirm plans for tomorrow. Most

EXIT LANE

Saturdays, I drop her off at the train before she teaches a half day of hot yoga, I go for a run and get in some work, and we reconvene over wings under a big-screen TV. Caroline and I met at Josie's on a Saturday afternoon when I pretended to care about Georgia football to get her to talk to me. It worked. And since then, we barely miss a game. Even though I still only know the names of half of the players.

At twenty-seven, most of my friends in Iowa have purchased homes with multiple garages for their multiple offspring, but in New York, with a place of my own and a medium-term girlfriend, I feel right on track.

The sex is hot. Caroline's friends are cool. Everything's going to plan at my big lawyer job with my big lawyer salary. When I accepted the new role, I told myself that after a few years, I'll probably be able to swing something remote—make my Iowa homecoming happen, but with a New York paycheck. It should feel more satisfying than it does. I add a new item to my mental checklist: Get comfortable with the reality that running into Marin won't, in fact, be a perk of this job.

MARIN

I don't think I've ever blushed before on a video call, but I do when the firm's managing partner introduces us. So does Teddy. "Marin, he went to Iowa, too. Small world. I'll connect you two over email." My breath is stuck somewhere in my throat, and I forget to unmute before I respond. "Sounds great. Hi, Teddy." Just as the next new hire is announced, my computer pings with a message. "Maybe it would have been smarter to bet on us never becoming colleagues?" It's like my body is back at Envy's Pub and his hand is tugging at my shirt, cementing a wager that felt more like a dare. Before I can reply, he writes again. "Take it easy on me. It's clear everyone here is as scared of you as I am." Then another message. "In a good way. Should I stop? I'm stopping."

Seeing his face, even thousands of miles away, recenters me. He's charming, poised, commanding—and trying to keep from laughing at his own notes to me during a company-wide Zoom. Maybe he can be a work crush. I mull the idea. Off-limits but just as much a part of office culture as P&L statements and annual reviews. A way to bring a little excitement and levity to an unending stream of serious meetings. I've never known how to safely categorize him, and perhaps this is his rightful place.

We start messaging throughout the day under the guise of seeking each other out for advice. Legal issues for me, internal office politics for him. One Friday, he asks out of the blue, "What does Gabby think about Copenhagen?" I'm making myself a cup of tea and write back immediately as the kettle screeches. "There's no Gabby. That's part of why I took the offer. I'm in the city at least once a month, but in the meantime, there was no one worth staying for—seemed like the right time to try something new."

"I thought New York was enough to keep you forever," he responds. Until very recently I thought the same.

EXIT LANE

After a few weeks of back-and-forth, there's too much to say during work hours, even if we straddle mine in Denmark and his in America. One night, after making a lengthy pros and cons list in my journal, I send an email with only a phone number in the body and the subject line "Colleagues, not friends."

That email led to a Saturday ritual we both refuse to acknowledge as one. Sometime after he sees Caroline off to hot yoga, Teddy dials my number and posts up at a park with his cold brew. I always wait four rings before picking up.

"Mar, you're not going to believe it." I'm chopping peppers for a gazpacho I'm pairing with my other big plan for the night: a *Sex and the City* season six rewatch in my pajamas. I picture Teddy somewhere on the Lower East Side, his face to the sun and his arms spread against the back of a bench. But the image is hazy. I haven't seen him below the neck since karaoke two years ago.

"Breaking news?" I ask as I open my cabinets, searching for a bowl to sweep my vegetables into. My storage space has doubled since I left New York, but most of it sits empty. Part of my relocation package from FourVC included a space of my choosing. As the youngest principal, and one of the only ones without kids and a mortgage, I was the obvious choice for a few years abroad. I surprised myself by warming to the idea almost immediately. As much as I love New York City, something about it, or who I was there, started feeling hollow to me. Things are different in Denmark. Here, in this light-wood palace with its sparse art, I realize how little time I spent at home before. That I prefer the solitude of an unfamiliar place to the loneliness of not recognizing myself in a familiar one.

"Ok, so—"

I cut him off, needling him. "Don't you want to ask me about my day? See what I got up to last night? Aren't you curious if I went out with anyone gorgeous?"

Teddy pauses. "Marin, I know exactly what you did last night. You logged off four hours later than you should have. You ate stovetop popcorn for dinner and took one of your 'cigarette walks' through the King's Garden before it closed at ten and came home to enjoy a massive bottle of mineral water and British home tours on YouTube."

I smile but refuse to validate this with a laugh. "Fair enough. Go on."

"Ok, so it's about Caroline." My spine straightens, and I try to stay focused on the tomatoes on my cutting board. I know her basic bio, but most of the time, she's a topic we skip over. "And I have to tell someone, and Carter is on a flight to see Sloane right now." *I'm his call after Carter.* My cheeks warm.

"We said 'I love you.'"

I set my knife down, taken aback by my own jealousy and sort of shocked by how it makes my face heat in a different way. "Of course she loves you. Didn't you make her a key to your apartment?" I try to be flip, to convince myself that both he and I already knew this to be true.

"Can we still acknowledge that this is a big deal?"

"I just think a fabricated sports alliance is a weird foot

EXIT LANE

to start a relationship on, that's all." I peel the cucumbers, wondering why I care at all.

"Ok, OK, forget I said anything. You are quite the relationship expert." He teases playfully, but I can't help the residual sting.

My life in Copenhagen is solitary, deliberately so. It's also supposed to be far away. From New York, and definitely from Iowa. The last person I think about before falling asleep isn't supposed to be from either of those lives. But Teddy's is the phone call I'm most excited to receive, even though I make a point to never save his number—my feckless resistance rendered hollow every time I dial it by memory or perk up whenever the 515 area code lights up my screen.

VIII

TEDDY

I spend all day waiting. Marin almost never calls me first, but she mentioned on Friday that she wanted my take on some due diligence before the end of the weekend. I've been on high alert ever since. Like a teenager, I turn my ringer volume all the way up and try to go about my day. Walking to pick up dry cleaning I'd forgotten about for months, I can't stop adding six hours to every passing minute. It's 10:04 p.m. for her. 10:07 p.m. 10:12 p.m. *She forgot or answered her question on her own*, I tell myself. *What is wrong with you that the highlight of your Sunday is the possibility of a work call?*

Just after five o'clock in New York, I'm home and contemplating a take-out order when my phone rings from my back pocket. I answer like it's an emergency.

"Is it snowing there?" she asks, her tone soft, devoid of her signature intensity.

"What's your weather app say?"

"Don't be an asshole. I'm homesick. Comfort me."

"There's snow in Copenhagen, if I'm not mistaken?"

"But it's not New York snow. It's too clean here. I mean,

EXIT LANE

it's a perfect city, and everyone's so hot, but there are no brown puddles of slush or late-night karaoke dives. I miss the messiness. I miss New York."

We're messy, I want to say. But instead I turn over her comment in silence. There's just the sound of me opening a beer and reclining on the sofa, my body going through the familiar motions while my head spins in every direction. Marin's never sentimental like this. She's devoid of longing or nostalgia. Then it hits me.

"Oh my god, Marin, you're high, aren't you?" In response, she unleashes her perfect, earth-pausing laugh, the one that's haunted me since that shitty bar in Illinois.

"Sue me, Teddy. I had a single square of mushroom chocolate two hours ago. And I'm not calling for legal advice. Is that OK?"

"It's fine." My heart quickens. "It's great. But it's late for you?"

"I stay up past my bedtime for a very select number of people. You're one of them."

Sometimes, when I can't sleep, I mentally play out the fantasy where she tells me it was always me, we repeat that kiss, and I am finally able to feel the press of her thighs against my hips. We throw a courthouse wedding with Carter and Sloane as witnesses and have a million more of these conversations without creating excuses to do so. All it takes is her telling me she likes staying up to talk to me for my mind to slip out of control and bolt off to an imagined distant future.

The snow colors the East River outside my windows a

shade of deep blue, and we fall into an easy conversation. We talk about the van Carter is renovating for his and Sloane's cross-country summer road trip. We don't discuss that both of us have kept these calls a secret from our best friends. I don't need Marin to admit she hasn't told Sloane because Carter would have brought it up with me if she had.

I realize I'm pacing at some point, desperate to channel all this excitement—this disbelief at the path we seem suddenly to be on—into something. When I mute my phone to pee, I try to ignore the oven flashing eight o'clock. Marin sounds more awake than she did earlier, somehow.

At almost nine, my phone drops to low battery, and I climb into bed to charge it and slip under the covers.

"If you really think about what's in a lake long enough, it will keep you from jumping off the dock." Marin's making her case for her distaste of large, still bodies of water. "I'm not saying that as a metaphor." I debate running to my closet to grab sweats but worry any sudden movements might shift the entire conversation, keep it from teetering at the edge of friendship. I burrow deeper under the blankets instead. She pauses mid-sentence. "Are you in bed?"

"It's where my charger is, Mar. I'm assuming you're in bed too. Even if I'm trying to keep myself from doing the plus-six time zone math because of how late it is for you."

"My sleep schedule . . . this doesn't bother me. I have this massive king here, and not to induce apartment envy, but it barely fills out my bedroom." I picture her curled up in one of those beds you see in Flatiron showroom

EXIT LANE

windows—all-white linen and fluffy pillows. I want to see her in it. Want to know what she wears to sleep. I picture boxer shorts, and I feel myself getting hard.

"My arm and leg can touch both bedroom walls from mine, so consider me jealous."

I'm not greedy enough to wish we were on a video call. Her voice is enough, more than enough. But I realize, in this moment, that I've been picturing her in my head this whole time, trying to conjure her, but my images of her are all years old or via work Zoom.

"Teddy, when was the last time we were together? Was it really karaoke?"

After that night, I promised myself I wouldn't let Marin go again, not the way I had when I dropped her off at her first apartment or when she slipped into a cab outside of Sing Sing. I owe it to every single sacred memory of the two of us to be honest.

"Marin, you know it was," I start. Then, afraid of spooking her, I sigh and pull back. "You took a chance on a Katy Perry song that very much did not pan out in your favor."

"I could say the exact same to you about the Paul Simon impersonation you did, but I won't, because I agreed to a Karaoke NDA, if you'll recall."

I have a retort at the ready, but I swallow it. *Tell her.* Having this window but not saying something, ruminating on it for another year—well, that feels worse than the risk of rejection. I close my eyes. "I wanted to kiss you so much that entire night, from the second I spotted you at Josie's. Every part of me was trying to be cool enough not to grab

75

your face in front of your very hot girlfriend and re-create the moment at that highway-exit dive bar."

There's silence, not the cold kind I'm used to from Marin on work calls when I can sense she thinks someone is stupid. This is something gentler. I can feel her contemplating the weight of her next move. If she hangs up on me, at least I got it off my chest, but where would that leave us? Whatever arousal I felt imagining her in bed has been bulldozed by the fear that I've toppled the first domino.

"Well, I probably wouldn't have kissed you," she starts. I'm gutted, red in the face in a dark room. I hear her readjusting her blankets, maybe turning on her side. "But I think about that dive bar all the time."

Relief floods my system. I'm not completely alone. Even if her feelings for me pale in comparison to mine for her. I fight the urge to make a joke. The tension is clear, but I know it's worth staying inside of it—how often do I have access to this side of Marin?

"I keep expecting another kiss to feel like that." I want to be honest without freaking her out. I worry I've gone too far.

"I think a lot of it was the nerves of moving to the city and being exhausted from the drive," she rationalizes. Then she pauses, and I steel myself to reply with "Of course" or "Right." But she's not done. "It was all those things, but it was also you, Teddy. Us."

My breath hitches. I could listen to her say my name over and over and over and find a new reason to rejoice every time. Fuck caution. I want all the risk associated with telling Marin how I really feel. Whatever strategy or

EXIT LANE

restraint I've been exercising hasn't worked thus far. I make the decision. I'm all in.

"Mar, I think about it every time I kiss someone for the first time. I always wonder if it'll feel as . . . earth-shattering as ours did." I wait, realizing my voice is shaking a little. "It never does."

"Not even with Caroline?" Her voice is lower, gravelly and perfect. It makes me shudder, the intimacy of it. I'm no longer imagining her a phone call away. She's here, next to me.

I feel enough shame that I can't say Caroline's name but not enough to keep from confessing. "It's only ever been you." My guilt is buried under the thrill of my proximity to the real, unarmored version of Marin. The part of her that's as hard to catch a glimpse of as unblemished New York City snow.

I close my eyes, taking in the moment one inhale, exhale at a time. The quiet doesn't scare me anymore. What terrifies me is what I hear myself say next, emboldened by the desire—the *need*—for Marin to know how close I feel to her even in her absence. "If we were together, right now, what would we be doing?"

IX

MARIN

"Disbelief" isn't the right word. I took the mushroom chocolate, and I waited. I'm the one who called Teddy. I didn't stop him when he started talking about that night at karaoke. Instead, I pulled the thread of the conversation further until we landed here. "Regret" isn't the right word, either. I wouldn't have pushed us to this place on my own, but something in me has uncoiled now that we've arrived.

Teddy's quiet on the other end of the line. Copenhagen's quiet, too. This time of night, there are the occasional bike tires whirling below. Every so often, an ambulance. I miss the din of New York, which I play from my phone on nights when the lack of sound gets too loud. I miss my gorgeous Tribeca apartment that is still shitty in some ways, as almost all New York apartments are. My cortado at the Elk. Walking down Canal into a summer Friday sunset. Making a guest bedroom out of sheets on my sofa for my sister. And tonight, I miss Teddy. A New York fixture for me even if I've only seen him there once.

I adjust the AirPods in my ears, nestling into the pile of down pillows propped up against my headboard. I hear

Teddy sigh, standing at a crossroads after deliberating. Am I smiling? It's almost as if there's no decision at all. For the first time, I start to wonder if this was always where we were going to end up.

"I wish we were together," he says. Normally, our banter is quick and clear. But tonight, his tone matches mine—slower, like every syllable counts. "Not at work or in that old car, but in the massive bed you're bragging about."

Fighting to ignore every instinct and move through the mental walls I've built to organize my life, I try to imagine another way. What if it was simple? What if how Teddy makes me feel—present and giddy and unencumbered—isn't something to work against?

I can already picture myself tomorrow morning, charting my plan to reconstruct my barricades. But tonight, as terrifying as it sounds, I just want to be here, with him.

I sink deeper under my covers, a hand mindlessly pulling at my pajama pants' drawstring. He's gravelly when he says, "I wish I was in bed with you, Marin Voss." I can picture him rubbing the back of his neck as he says it.

I'm lightheaded, dazed by how one sentence can unlock something in me. Teddy wants me. I can't pretend it's news, but hearing the words, I have to acknowledge how much I want Teddy, too.

Ignoring the creep of early morning, I make a decision of my own. "If we were together—" I pause, noticing my index finger tracing the edges of my underwear. My breathing hitches. "I'd want you to be naked. It's strange that we've never seen each other without clothes on, isn't it?" I'm emboldened by something, using all my strength to push away thoughts of pragmatism and control.

"Considering we're—and these are your words, not mine—'strictly colleagues,' I don't think it's that strange," he says. "I never—" He cuts himself off, and his voice deepens. "I'm sorry. I'm nervous." His laugh is like an exhale between us, easing the tension just enough for him to continue. "I'd give anything to see you naked, Marin. To see how much you're like what I've imagined."

My feelings, stuffed down and stifled for all these years, flood my body with warmth. My body tenses, then loosens. My jaw unclenches, and my legs splay open, the way they always do when I touch myself. I can almost remember his scent, inches from his face in that karaoke room, all those hours in the car. "I'm nervous, too," I whisper back. "But I wouldn't be if you were actually here. Something about being around you makes me feel like we've always known each other." Teddy is grinning. I can almost see it. My chin tilts, his imaginary finger lifting it to his face. "That feeling unlocks something in me. And it terrifies me."

"Me too." He sighs. We could still retrace our steps, call it a fluke, pretend the conversation never happened. But he goes on.

"I think about our kiss all the time. Most days," he says. "It feels so juvenile—I never think about any other kiss—but that one plays on repeat like a movie scene for me."

The tiniest sigh escapes my throat as I lift my hips and slip my underwear and pajama pants off, bunching them

EXIT LANE

under the covers. "I think about it, too. I half expected you to come knocking at my hotel room. For the two of us to fuck that night." Maybe there's a more eloquent way to slam the door of plausible deniability than the word "fuck," but I can't think of it, not in this state.

"Trust me, Marin, I wanted to. Had to settle for jerking off thinking about you down the hall. More than once that night. You had me so worked up I couldn't sleep until I got you out of my system. Only I've never been able to get you out of my fucking system." Blood rushes between my legs at the thought. In my head, he's here, his thumb brushing across my lips, trailing down my neck, skimming across my nipples that are pressing against the ribbed cotton of my tank top. I suck in a shallow breath, and I know he can hear it, register the nature of my reaction to his confession.

"That kiss made me feel like a teenager," I whisper. "So does this." I cringe at myself. Not because it isn't true—that the heady feelings I get around him aren't real—but because for me, thoughts of those years bring up weeks of hospice, waves of grief. I push myself to be present. To be here in this new feeling, even though it's uncharted. To experience Teddy as something other than part of the life I left behind. All I want is to give in to him completely, to tell him he's on my mind all the time and that I want him in every way imaginable, but that's a leap I'm not ready for. I settle for the silence of our breathing, growing heavier by the moment. I settle for his voice in my sheets.

"If I was in Copenhagen, naked in your king-size bed, I would kiss you again."

I reach for a pillow, stuffing it under my hips, feeling myself open at the thought.

He keeps going. "This time, I wouldn't stop there."

My fingers slip between my legs, tentatively touching a part of myself that feels safe. I'm trying to ignore the intruding thoughts that insist on reminding me I'm having phone sex with someone I have to see at an all-hands meeting.

"I'd pull you close enough so you could feel how much I want you. How much I've always wanted you." His nostalgic tone would normally be a turnoff. Not tonight. "Marin, you wouldn't believe how hard I am just thinking about you right now."

I touch myself, uninclined to reach for a vibrator, focused instead on superimposing Teddy's hand on mine. His palm bracing against my hip. His fingers teasing me, touching me everywhere but not giving me enough.

I squeeze my eyes shut, picture us, and describe what I see. "If we were together, I'd press you against me so you could feel how wet you make me." At once, I realize all the times I've imagined some version of this and shoved those visions away in favor of something I deemed safer. Something that asked for less of me. It's as if all the bottled desire has nowhere to go but here. "Fuck, Teddy, how wet you're making me."

"I want to go down on you for hours. I don't want to stop until I know the taste of you so well that I can call it to mind whenever I want." I feel my shoulders digging into the mattress, fighting for purchase against all this longing.

"Teddy." It's all I can get out, but I know it's enough.

"I wanted to pull over on I-80 and rip that fucking button-down off of you. That stupid black bra."

I bring my other hand to my breast, picturing him kissing my neck while the heat builds.

"You are the most beautiful thing." He says it like a fact, without hesitation. "I can't imagine wanting anyone more."

I come, my entire torso shaking, letting myself go without concern for what I sound like or what it might mean for us. I come as a release, something pent-up unspooling from the place where my hips stretch open. It's bigger than fear. It's deeper than lust. My body lands me right here, breathless in my bed, desperately trying to understand how I would survive being with Teddy in real life if this is what phone sex with him does to me.

"Fuck, Marin," he whispers. "I want to keep that sound."

"It's yours, Teddy. You earned it. You made me come, made me make that sound, without even putting your mouth on me."

He gasps, my name a strained noise deep in his throat. I pull the comforter over my head. Already, there's an awkwardness, somehow palpable in the space between us. Or maybe it's a feeling I'm not used to. Vulnerability. I listen to our breaths, letting the sound anchor me.

"I loved talking to you, Mar." My eyes prickle that he knows I can't handle anything more pointed than that.

I feel turned inside out, the soft belly of my longing for Teddy exposed. I don't have the energy to make a list of the reasons why he's not right, why our lives could never coalesce, why this warm, unthreatening man scares the shit out of me.

"I loved talking to you, too." I wipe my eyes. "Goodnight, Teddy." I hang up before he responds, check the time—3 a.m.—and toss my phone across the bed.

X

TEDDY

Physically, I'm present. I'm bantering with my favorite bartender and cheering in the general direction of the single TV behind the bar. But it took me a very long, very cold shower and two espressos to even get me to Josie's today. My foamy Guinness is sitting neglected in front of me, and Caroline is to my left, talking with her friends about their annual summer weekend in the Ozarks. I excuse myself to the bathroom, smiling politely while my head spins.

For six days now, I've tried to convince myself it wasn't cheating. That I love Caroline, just like I told her I do. That I'm in a healthy relationship, the kind I've always pictured for myself. So what if she doesn't make my heart beat out of my chest? Stability and swooning are incompatible.

I look into the mirror with as much conviction as I can muster in the dim light. Sunday was a fluke. It was an accident without any ties to reality or any meaning beyond the hours in which it transpired. Pressing my forearm against the wall as if to prop me up, I run the night back, starting from the beginning, examining my case, leaning toward innocence, but willing myself to review every piece of relevant evidence. I focus on the letter of the law and ignore the spirit of it as I try to steady myself. Before I reach any conclusion, someone knocks on the bathroom door, and I am forced to abandon my shame spiral.

When the game's over, Caroline suggests dinner at a cozy French spot she likes, and I don't know how to say no. I feel like I'm on a rooftop, watching the two of us walking down the street from a great height. After settling into our corner table, Caroline reaches for both of my hands, without a hint of urgency. "You're distant," she says, pulling away to brush her curtain bangs off her face. She gives me a forced smile. "And I know why."

I reel. She went through my phone. Marin said something to her. Does Marin even know her last name? Is Caroline's email on the CorePower "Meet our Instructors" page? I can hear my favorite 1L professor loud and clear. "Let people tell you what they perceive as truth before you have the chance to ruin it for yourself by speaking too soon." I listen, pulling my sweating palms into my lap.

"It's about the lake weekend," she continues. "It was sweet of Shannon to say something about you maybe coming this year—I'd love that—but I know it's a commitment, and you want to get to Iowa and everything. I don't want you to think there's pressure." She looks proud, like she can't wait to tell her therapist about how she handled this. I want her to be right. For both of us.

I sigh into my bistro chair and nod gratefully to the waiter pouring our wine. "Lakes. So much stagnant water." She grimaces, then tries to pass it off as a laugh. Eager to

EXIT LANE

move past this. Ideally, for me to tell her that of course I'll come.

I look at her, really look at her. Caroline is the right woman for me, for my dreams. I can see my future with her so clearly, and it's the one I've always envisioned: We'd date for another year, move in together. I'd propose with a ring from that designer she always points out when we walk past the shop on Bleecker Street. Our wedding would be at the Des Moines Art Center, and we'd be settled on Fifty-First Street in no time.

But when the waiter comes back for our order, I politely wave him off. Caroline's face tightens. My mouth goes dry. From some place beyond my rational mind, I hear myself say, "Actually, there's something else I need to talk to you about." Caroline nods, draining the rest of her glass as my vision blurs into bokeh. "Caroline, you're incredible, and what we have . . ." *Say it.* "It's not forever for me. It's, um . . ."

I stop myself before I say something dumb just to fill the air or make myself feel better. I brace for tears, maybe indignation. I realize I haven't appropriately prepared for a reaction at all because thirty seconds ago, I was convinced I could make this relationship work, by force or by forgetting.

She laughs sharply, pushing her hair off her shoulder. Her eyes are hurt, surprised, even, but not angry. "Ok. Also, obviously, you're in love with the girl in Sweden." She reaches for my upper arms, gripping them like she does to her drunk girlfriends when they're trying to text an ex and they need some sense talked into them. I'm being condescended to, and honestly, I deserve it.

"Denmark."

An eye roll from her, an exhale from me, one that starts to rearrange something in me on a cellular level. I realize I didn't deny it. I realize how nice it feels to not refute it.

"I just thought . . ." She shakes her head and stands up. Gives me a good, long, defiant stare before putting on her coat. "I hope someone someday is as obsessed with me as you are with her to throw away something this good." My shoulders slump. I want to comfort her, and before I get a chance to fumble for words, I realize the most comforting thing I can do right now is shut up.

"I'm glad you were honest. I'm not going to be anyone's backup plan." Over her shoulder as she walks to the door: "Might as well go after her at this point."

MARIN

All week, I think about talking to Sloane about what happened, but I can't bring myself to make the call. I hate being messy, and I have a physical reaction to the idea that Sloane—or Sloane and Carter—might have to clean up after me.

The workweek is a treasured distraction, and I throw myself into it, shoving the incident into the recesses of my mind—mostly successfully—until Sunday morning. I bike thirty minutes through the slushy snow to Vesterbro, seeking punishment from a Pilates reformer. In class, I fixate on what Teddy said about our one and only kiss. I struggle

EXIT LANE

to focus on wrapping my abs or releasing the tension in my poses, thinking instead about the sound he made when he heard me come. During cooldown, I replay how he described jerking off in his hotel room thinking about me.

Our instructor thanks us with a slight bow. I tug on my snow boots. The day stretches out in front of me. The last thing I want to do is be home, pressing rewind on our conversation one more time. It happened. It doesn't matter. It was a phone call across an ocean, practically a fever dream.

I need a walk. I need cold air. I need other images to replace the ones of Teddy swirling in my head.

I make my way to Copenhagen Contemporary. As I wander through the galleries, my phone rings. My sister, Violet. I stop in my tracks, jolted by a flash of anxiety that hits me whenever I hear from her at odd hours. I answer.

"Mar, I miss you." Before I can ask why she's even awake, she jumps in. "Tell me how you're doing, but this time, try not to mention anything about work."

I laugh, darting behind a video installation and leaning against a wall to avoid the judgment of being on my phone. "I'm good. Tired, maybe a little homesick." Not a lie, but not exactly the truth. Since our dad's passing, protecting Violet became my biggest priority. That means making sure she always has money for flights back to Iowa, someone she can call no matter what, and nothing to worry about when it comes to me.

"I miss Iowa all the time." Violet is wistful. I can't relate. She has no idea what that place has come to mean to me, only that I've never dreamed of going back.

"You'll always have Iowa." I try my best to make that sound like a good thing. "I'm glad you're in Chicago, though. There's so much opportunity there for you. And so many frat boys."

Violet laughs at my running gag about her taste in men. Then she pauses the way she always does before saying something she's scared to get out. "Are you OK in Copenhagen? Why are you even . . ." She sighs. "Sometimes you seem like you're not OK. And I worry about you."

It's the thing I dread hearing from her—that I'm a source of anything but comfort. But for the first time, I am tempted to tell her the truth: that I'm lonely. That I keep running farther and farther away. That I think I might be in love with someone who hits way too close to home.

But I can't. I transform back into the measured older sister she deserves. "I'm settling in here, V, and it's not forever. You know, I have a few friend coffee dates next week, so things are shaping up. And I can't wait for you to come. But listen, I'm at an art museum. Let me call you back when I get home."

After we hang up, I feel relief, like I've successfully passed off a white lie. Then the loop of Teddy's voice kicks back in, and a few blocks from home, I start mentally calculating minus-six time zones. Teddy is probably still asleep, in bed with Caroline. He'll probably pick up Russ & Daughters for the two of them, even though the Sunday line will be maddening, and go for a run. He'll call Carter or his mom and reminisce about old times. I tell myself that Teddy's not thinking about me. And I should try my best not to think about him.

XI

TEDDY

To: teddy.mccarrel@iowauniversity.edu
From: mv@fourvc.com
Subject line: Going forward

Teddy—
Upon reflection, I'd like to apologize for my behavior a few weeks ago. I've decided it's best to limit our interactions as much as possible. It's better for both of us and everyone else involved.

Thank you for understanding.

Best,
MV

I've memorized the email I woke up to on Monday. I hate the way my stomach tightens at "both of us" every single time. How I hold my breath at "everyone else involved" and its invocation of Caroline and Carter and Sloane and I don't even know who else. Our colleagues? Every temptation I have to call Marin and talk her into reconsidering is met with an equally strong pang of embarrassment.

"God, Teddy, you can be so dumb. And lovable, but very

stupid." Carter and I are on the phone the next day while I walk from the office to the gym. Turns out, my commitment to leaving him in the dark about Marin expired as soon as I broke up with Caroline. There was no way of explaining to my best friend why I ended things with someone I'd described as "wife material" without also telling him about the illicit phone sex with his girlfriend's best friend. In as little detail as possible.

I'm pacing in front of a bodega now. "Am I really the guy who has a not-even-hookup with someone and then breaks up with his long-term girlfriend? Who could ever take me seriously?"

"You feel something for her, Ted, like enough to end a perfectly solid relationship. Listen, the cheating stuff . . . is sensitive for you, and maybe you did this with Marin to force yourself into an out with Caroline." I stop, considering his analysis. He might be right. Carter's always been better at the emotional conversations that I'd rather sweep under the rug, and he often knows me better than I know myself. "I'm not telling you to do anything brash like fly to Copenhagen and profess your love, but it's worth paying attention to the way you feel—especially with everything you have going on. It's a lot."

He's referencing the other thing in my life that I've told only him, the other thing I'd rather sweep under the rug: that one doctor referred me to another doctor who is running some tests. That I'm young and healthy and the odds are low, but it's worth checking some things out to be safe. That even seeing the word "oncology" in an email

EXIT LANE

and leaning back for an MRI is enough to make me want to reconsider the way I'm moving through my life.

The second I hang up, I feel something start to crystallize in my head, in my chest, in the recesses of my gut. It grows stronger and stronger until it's wrapped around every inch of me, full-body clarity like I've only felt one other time in my life, when my mom told us my dad was moving to a hotel for a few weeks while they figured things out. Then it was rage, and now it's an equally singular and blinding emotion: determination.

Nothing seems as complicated as I've told myself it was since I first saw Marin on campus. She's the person I think about all the time. My first instinct whenever I pick up my phone is to call her. When we're talking, it's hard to remember why I let this cloud of confusion drive me to inaction for all these years. When we're together, it's the only thing that matters.

I look up from my pacing and realize I'm walking past Sing Sing. A dumb smile lands on my face. I don't care about what's rational or all the reasons why letting her go might be logical. All that matters is Marin, getting to her, and giving what we've tried to ignore a real shot.

MARIN

I log off of my last call just in time for my sushi delivery. It's Wednesday. Two days since I sent the email. I've hired a Danish tutor to distract me. She's strict and incredibly unforgiving. I'm being whipped into shape via vocab lessons, and it's good for me. I matched with a gorgeous producer on Raya, but his messages make me want to drop my phone in the toilet. "We'd make the ultimate power couple" and a string of arm muscle emojis. My first thought? To tell Teddy about it. Instead, I swipe again.

I take my salmon rolls out to the terrace. It's freezing, but the gentle whir of Copenhagen at night is starting to win me over. Wrapped in a mohair throw and a beanie Sloane's mom gave me five Christmases ago, I try to convince myself I made the right decision. That cutting Teddy off was the only option. That Teddy reminds me too much of what I once thought I'd want when I grew up. A close family. A home I could always come back to. I lost all that when I was fifteen. The life I rebuilt is different, distant, and as far away from the pain as possible. It's a life that looks good, but most of the time, it doesn't feel like anything at all.

And yet, as much distance as I've put between myself and my old hurt, when I'm unable to sleep or distracted in meetings, it's Teddy's face I see. His corn-fed, Midwestern-mannered, quick-to-laugh face.

I pull the blanket over my head like a hood, shivering, and turn back to the plate in my lap.

Mid-bite, I hear a knock. Only police and Jehovah's Witnesses show up at your door in Denmark. Privacy is sacred here.

Another knock. I stand, the cold through my socked feet multiplying my nerves. I close the balcony door gently, grab my phone from the kitchen table, and preemptively

EXIT LANE

dial the local emergency number. My heart beats in my throat. The quiet of the night I was charmed by takes on hostility. I grab a skillet off my stove, a fine weapon in case I need it. One hand ready to dial, another clenching cookware, I try to recall the thirty-minute self-defense class FourVC held during a work retreat. I plant my feet, swing the door open, and immediately stumble back. Like I've been pummeled by a wave. Like being pulled under by the tide is all I've really wanted.

XII

TEDDY

Seeing her in pajamas makes the eight hours in Comfort Plus next to a chatty toddler feel worth it. Her hair's slipping out of a braid, and one pant leg is tucked into a pushed-down sock. This isn't the Marin I work with every day. This is the Marin I haven't been able to get out of my head for the last five years.

I imagined this reunion unfolding a thousand different ways—immediate sex in the kitchen, intruding on someone else having sex with Marin in the kitchen, awkward silence, a curt request to turn around immediately. My logical brain settled on Marin responding in her signature style, with a lot of questions in a raised tone. The skillet in her hand? No amount of daydreaming could have prepared me for that.

And her warmth, that feeling of being in her presence—I think I forget what it's like, as a coping mechanism.

I rock back and forth from heel to toe in the same tennis shoes I was wearing when I hatched this plan. Let her process. Don't overwhelm her any more than you already have.

She's speechless, sputtering while she pushes up her sleeves and scans me, suitcase and all, before

EXIT LANE

whisper-shouting, "Teddy, why didn't you call? Or email me? Are you here . . . just to see me? Or for something else? Why didn't I know you'd be standing here right now?"The list of questions comes out in a jumble. I watch her toggle between what she feels and what she wants to feel. She sets the skillet down on a nearby credenza. A smile works its way out of the corner of her perfect mouth, but then she crosses her arms.

She's apprehensive, but the grin's winning where she's trying desperately to stay stern.

There was no point in rehearsing anything. The second I'm in front of Marin, I can only say exactly what I feel. I whisper in her hallway, leaning against the doorframe.

"This is a romantic gesture, Mar. That's why I didn't text you my flight confirmation number." If I could just kiss her, lift the pajama top off her shoulders and make good on where we left our phone conversation off.

She winces at the word "romantic," but a subtle blush spreads across her face, too, and it's like she's read my mind. Annoyed, she reaches one hand for the doorframe, bristling as she grazes my fingers and decides crossing her arms is much safer. I watch her run through her response in her head, seeing the way her eyes avoid mine as she constructs a cost-benefit analysis in real time. "You can't just show up here and expect me to go back on what I said, Teddy. What we did wasn't right. You're in a relationship. We work together. I . . . live here." A neighbor slips out of their door with the poshest-looking dog I've ever seen. They both glare at us.

97

Marin sighs. "Come in."

The apartment is somewhere on the opposite end of the spectrum of the rundown place I've clung to since the two of us first rolled into New York five years ago. The ceilings shoot past twenty feet. The walls are wood paneled, even in the bathroom, where I notice a clawfoot tub as we walk by. An office, without a hideous monitor and computer chair from Amazon. Throw blankets that look like they were chosen specifically for this space and seem to know it. It's intimidating, like every single part of her life. But the closer I get to the real Marin, the more confident I feel that the rigid organization, the shininess of it all, is just an attempt at control.

Before I can stop myself, I'm picturing our life here, in this apartment. Marin doesn't want the house on Fifty-First Street and T-ball games at the same park where Carter and I met, but maybe I could want this. If it means having her. Before I can examine the thought, fear seeps in. If I don't clutch that dream I've pinned my future on, where does it leave me? *Be here*, I remind myself, a mantra I stole from one of Caroline's morning meditations months ago.

Marin puts on a kettle, leaning against her spotless marble counter. Her arms seem permanently crossed at this point, so I try to explain.

"It's over with Caroline," I tell her, inching toward the kitchen like I'm approaching a cornered animal. "I broke up with her. Before you sent the email. And I'm not saying that to pressure you or demand that this"—insert erratic pointing between the two of us—"has to become . . . anything

EXIT LANE

more than it is. But I decided I had to at least create the opportunity to give it a chance."

Saying it, I feel instantly lighter. Watching her process the news about Caroline, about my unwillingness to ignore this thing we have, I feel hope flutter somewhere in my chest. She doesn't respond, just carries two mugs that seem to shimmer in the low light over to her dining table. With her sitting across from me, I'm struck by how little time we've spent in the same room. In contrast to our hours on the phone and the nights I've spent alone imagining what this would feel like, there's been so little actual face-to-face interaction. And maybe I should be grateful for whatever amount of sober thinking that distance has granted me. Because her beauty, even at her most calculated and cold, is arresting in real life, and it engulfs me. Perfect posture. A pajama shirt undone one button too low. Those cheekbones sprinkled with freckles and the way she runs her finger across her collarbone when she's thinking. The way she slides her hair behind her ear.

I wrest my eyes away from her gestures and press my palms into the warm mug. "Here's what I'm proposing, and I'm sorry I don't have a deck to go along with this." She nods, not taking the bait on my attempt at a joke. I'm overcompensating for my uncertainty. I'm scared to stop talking because she could very well ask me to book the next flight back to New York, so I go on. "I'll get a hotel nearby for the week. We'll hang out as little or as much as you want. And by the end of the trip, we'll decide if what happened on the phone that night means anything. Worst-case scenario:

It's awkward, and we endure next year's FourVC offsite in Portugal with the help of a lot of wine. Best-case scenario: Well, I don't know. That's kind of what I'm here to find out."

My beating heart fills the silence in the room. It's high risk, but so was flying out here in the first place. So was not taking action at all. I'll do anything she asks. Even if these ten minutes are all I get with her, it's proof enough that no other person has ever made me feel this way, and I'm willing to bet no one else ever will. She uncrosses her arms, and I don't dare blink. Marin opens her mouth, pulls an inhale, and presses her head into her hands like they might help her think.

"Teddy, this is a lot to take in." I brace for impact, certain she's about to send me right back to the airport. "And I know you're jet-lagged, so maybe it doesn't feel like it, but it's late. Can I make the bed in the office, and we can talk about it in the morning?"

Less enthusiastic a response than kitchen sex, but I can work with it. My entire body relaxes at the thought of at least another day with her. "That's perfect. Thank you."

Silently slipping from her seat, Marin pulls some sheets from a burl wood wardrobe, tossing me a towel with her initials embroidered on the side. In the shower, I try to convince myself that coming here was right, that there's a world in which I leave Denmark knowing if Marin and I could ever be something. With a towel around my waist, I discover a cream daybed wrapped in striped sheets with a tiny chocolate placed on my pillow. I interpret the hotel turndown service as an olive branch and fall asleep grinning.

EXIT LANE

MARIN

Teddy McCarrel, arms splayed and draped off the edges of my guest bed, in my apartment. It's like seeing a ghost, except this apparition falls victim to morning wood and audible snoring. The light falls across his face from where I stand in the doorway. He's just so Teddy. Of course he flew here. Of course he thinks we can power through years of attachment theory work in a week. Of course his dick is huge. The way his mouth dips open in his sleep, his lips soft. He's beautiful. And brash. I'm trying not to stare at the abs that lead to the sturdy hip bones that are somewhere near his cock, straining against a pair of poplin pajama pants. It registers as a stirring between my legs nonetheless. He's borderline otherworldly in this setting. And I need a coffee before I do something stupid.

"You knew about this?" I ask as sternly and quietly as I can into my phone. I'm in the kitchen soft-scrambling eggs and doing my best to hold off on the espresso machine until Teddy's awake. It's the middle of the night for Sloane—and technically for him too—but I knew she'd answer. That getting a call like this is an actual bucket-list item for her, one informed by a steady diet of '90s rom-coms and an emotionally withholding best friend.

"To be clear, Carter knew about this. I had no idea until Teddy landed. Not that I disapprove. I just think it's a little reckless on his part." Before I can interrupt, she self-edits. "But charming. Just go easy on him, OK? Or just have the incredible, pent-up sex you both needed to have and then break his heart, I guess. Which is more your speed."

"Sloane, I don't like surprises." I'm shocked at the vulnerability in my voice. She's heard it before, about my family, but never my love life. I lift myself onto the counter, resting my socked foot on the island, pressing my head back into the cabinet, face to the skylight above. Undulating between excitement and apprehension, part of me wishes I'd never let him into the apartment. But another part of me can't believe the luck of him being here. That he did the bold thing that I never would have done.

"Mar, babe, I know you don't. And I know you have a whole plan about marrying a wealthy eighty-five-year-old in New York and never coming back to the Midwest ever again. I get it. But there's a man asleep in your apartment who adores you almost as much as I do, despite you giving him almost nothing to work with over the last five years." She's right, per usual.

"You know I can't end up with Teddy," I sputter before I can stop myself. "It can't be that easy. Anything that easy comes with a catch."

"I'm not your therapist, although, you know, Jessica is doing God's work. But I will remind you that maybe some things can be easy. We were easy, right? You took a chance on me, and look at us. Try to go easy on yourself too. And maybe open yourself up to the slight possibility that Teddy could be the love of your life? Just an idea."

I grumble out something about calling her later, and I hate that she can tell she made headway with me. That she'll be too excited about it to fall back asleep right away.

I send a note to the office, letting my partners know

EXIT LANE

I'll be taking the day, which they'll all be pleased by. It's been a year or so since I took a proper vacation, and I've grown accustomed to stacking my weekend with the kind of appointments normal people take during work hours. It's a badge of honor to leave my unlimited PTO untouched. Though I suspect the badge is revoked as soon as I spend any time examining why that matters to me.

Lounging on my sofa, desperate for coffee and further explanation from Teddy, I start to wonder what mornings would feel like if I didn't start working from my phone in bed. I could read a book from the pile I've accumulated from my local bookstore or finish a crossword from the care package my mom sent.

But the stillness starts to creep me out. I slip on my Levi's, a massive sweater, and the Max Mara coat I bought myself with my last year-end bonus and grab my keys. The cold air works its magic, and I'm determined to take at least some of Sloane's advice. On my bike, pedaling to Andersen & Maillard, it feels good to get into my body. To remember I have limbs and lungs, that I'm not just a brain and the worry that comes with it. I order a cortado. Two sticky buns. A loaf of sourdough. More espresso beans. I'm on my way back, certain that despite the time change, Teddy will be awake, and now I'm ready for him.

XIII

TEDDY

I wake up with a sore back, a dead phone, and a Zen-like calm I haven't felt in years. The sun is warm, casting a pale light across the office. I tiptoe over to Marin's desk, wiggle a mouse to check the time, and see that it's almost noon and that—according to an OOO notification that pops up on the screen—she took the day off. Marin Voss has taken exactly zero vacation since I started working with her. I count my wins: She didn't kick me out. She isn't dismissing me for work. In the kitchen, there's a carafe of water with a matching cup and a note on the counter: "Be back soon x MV." Marin's handwriting, the way it flops to the right somewhere between print and script, puts a stupid grin on my face. That I get to see it at all feels like we've unlocked some new level of closeness, earned or not. I'm buzzing as I settle at a barstool. *Things could work out*, I dare to think. This could be the moment we look back at in forty years, the fulcrum in the story where everything changed.

In the bathroom, Marin's left a D.S. & Durga candle burning over the toilet, and I instantly recognize the scent

EXIT LANE

as the perfume she wears. Or at least, the perfume she wore five years ago.

I am in desperate need of another shower after hours of tossing and turning while trying to force my body onto Copenhagen time, to keep it from picking apart every single gesture Marin made and every syllable she uttered since I arrived. Under the steady stream of hot water, I give up on collecting my thoughts. I'm here because I think I might be in love with Marin. Or at least, I'm here to find out if I could be. If the entire thing blows up in my face, at least I'll know I tried. Maybe then I can finally let go of this crush I've harbored for most of my adult life.

Thoughts at top volume, I wrap myself in another towel and walk back toward my makeshift accommodations. I turn the corner in the hall, and as I slow in front of a Wolfgang Tillmans exhibition poster—*how did we never talk about both seeing this?*—I promptly slip on the hard-wood floor. I am on the ground, at the feet of Marin Voss, wrapped in a camel coat, carrying what smells like pastries. Seminaked, I look up at her expecting to see something smug cross her beatific face. At my clumsiness. At my presence at all.

But instead, Marin can't stop laughing, dropping her bags to the counter and stabilizing herself against the wall. "It's . . . it's so funny, in a slipping-on-a-banana-peel way. That you're here at all. I'm sorry, are you OK?" She pulls me up, and for a second, we're inches away. My chest damp and heaving. The belt of her coat undone. I notice her pajama shirt from the night before, still so goddamn unbuttoned. Her cheeks are flushed from being in the cold. The afternoon sun streams into the room with full force, lighting up a face I've only seen on a computer camera for the last two years. She does that hair-tuck thing, reenacting a moment I can't stop replaying in my head from the road trip, and I realize I am getting hard underneath her monogrammed towel, which is possibly the only thing that could make this situation more awkward.

"Nothing to see here." I stand taller and rewrap my towel.

Her eyes flit to my waist, and she rests her hand on my bare shoulder and leans to speak into my ear. "Breakfast when you're ready."

She's cheerful, maybe even flirtatious. Enough so that I momentarily consider pressing her against the wall, yanking the belt of her coat, and kissing her for the second time in my life.

But if I want this trip to be more than one kiss or the culmination of our phone sex session, there's talking to do first.

I scuttle into the office to change into a sweatshirt and pants with wool socks. The whirl of the espresso machine strikes me as intimate in a way it never has before, and I realize there's been a pair of rose-colored glasses permanently affixed to my face since the moment I walked through Marin's door. Well, probably the moment I spent $4,000 on a last-minute ticket. Making the decision to ignore the voicemail from my doctor that came in during the flight, I tell myself that everything else can wait. Some-one stop me. I'm an optimist on the loose.

MARIN

"I assume you take yours with milk and sugar?" I ask, hand-ing him a mug of my dad's so precious to me that I wrapped it in two cashmere sweaters and transported it in my carry-on when I moved.

"And yours is black still, I presume?"

I laugh, then blush—that we would both recall these details from the one time we had coffee together, procured from a motel lobby in suburban Illinois and consumed along I-294.

He slides into the chair across from mine, eyes bright and eager. Seeing Teddy in daylight, not across a screen, I can catalog how he's changed and how he hasn't. He's grown into his features. He still carries himself with confidence, but it's more relaxed, less straight-backed.

I wish he'd stop staring at me with those eyes. And I wish I could focus on something other than the way his shoulders are pressing against his cotton sweatshirt. I never feel nervous on dates—not that this qualifies as one—and I'm not big on morning-after hangs. This is novel. I'm glad Teddy's the first person I'm making breakfast for. In a weird way that I'm not sure how to interrogate yet, it feels right.

I tried to make a pros and cons list in my journal this morning, before calling Sloane, but the competing thoughts were so disorienting that I shoved the notebook away like it was to blame. I'm determined to try my best not to analyze my feelings to death, not to let my rational mind hijack the day.

And now I have Teddy here in the flesh to help with that. The scene of him sleeping, shirtless with an erection. His chiseled body fresh from the shower, in accidental repose on my floor. Now, watching him watch me, my rational mind is no longer a factor. All I can think about is enacting every scene from our phone call here on the kitchen counter. That has to mean something. But does it matter? I straighten my spine and push my hair out of my face, the way I always do when I'm nervous. No one else makes me feel this way. What if I let myself think of that as a good thing?

Stop belaboring it, I tell myself. *You've already decided you're letting him stay.*

"Does your surprise trip come with a surprise agenda?" I ask.

Teddy smiles. "The only game plan was to not get thrown out of your apartment. I saw you took the day off."

I smooth the linen tablecloth mindlessly, moved by the eagerness in his voice. That he wanted to ask more but didn't. This time, we're not stuck on the interstate with a broken radio. We have the entire city of Copenhagen at our disposal.

"Here's the plan. Sloane's visiting in two weeks with Violet for her spring break. I'm going to test run a trial itinerary on you."

EXIT LANE

Teddy leans back in his chair, and I feel something warm in the middle of my hips.

"You're telling me Marin Voss is looking for some constructive feedback? I'm in."

"We leave in thirty," I instruct, tossing back my cortado. Trying to swallow a feeling stronger than a crush, sweeter than desire.

XIV

TEDDY

I stifle a massive yawn while mimicking Marin's stance, arms crossed behind her back, as we stand in front of a burgundy hall stuffed with statues at the Thorvaldsens Museum. "Teddy, are you with me?"

I nod, but I also can't keep from laughing. My body doesn't know what time it is, but it knows that watching Marin moonlight as a tour guide is sexy, even if I could probably be a bit more engaged with what she's showing me.

"Oh my god, you hate this. Of course you hate this." She moves her hand to the sleeve of my coat, her concern genuine. I'm here, but in my head, there's nothing between her skin and mine. We're back at the apartment, making up for lost time.

I interrupt, eager for her to know that wherever she is, is exactly where I want to be. "No, not at all, I'm just a little . . ."

Her tone shifts, and I recognize this tenor from meetings where she plays moderator for dozens of finicky investors. "You're a modern art guy. Naturally. I'm noting the

EXIT LANE

Japanese denim and APC wool trench you're wearing. Ok, come on. We're pivoting."

Does she know I'd follow her anywhere, and should I be embarrassed by that? I wonder. To see her act the way she does on the phone and in work calls in real life is almost intimidatingly thrilling. Twelve hours into this grand romantic gesture, and I'm captivated by how much more spectacular she is up close—even more than I remember. And I'm floored by how full-body smitten I am in her proximity.

Marin checks her phone and scrunches her nose. "We have twenty minutes to make a train. You ready to book it?"

As I trail her through the streets of Copenhagen, past unaccompanied babies napping in strollers and quaintly tidy trash cans, I can see the city's appeal. Maybe I could live here. Maybe it's as good a place to raise kids as Iowa is. Isn't that what people say about Denmark? Good for families? The thoughts flash through my mind without warning, and I shake my head as if that will set them free.

We arrive at the station out of breath, and Marin punches instructions into a touchscreen machine, buys our tickets, and whisks us onto the metro. Not a subway car jammed full of deodorant-averse teenagers and the occasional hot-boxing weed-smoker like I'm used to. A silent train bullet-ing through the countryside with passengers whispering respectfully and sipping tea from thermoses.

"It gets dark here at, like, four, so time is of the essence," Marin explains once we settle into seats facing each other. Our knees knock accidentally, but then they stay there, resting against each other. Marin raises a hand, a motion I've seen her make before in meetings. She's about to ask an uncomfortable question.

"Just so we're aligned," she starts, then sighs. "Sorry, I don't know why I'm in work mode right now." She pauses, and I see the genuine concern in her movements. She fumbles in her bag for her mints, pops one, and offers the tin to me.

It hits me: What I came here seeking is as much of a risk for her as it is for me. She's so poised and frank that I sometimes forget that her underbelly is as soft as mine. Even if glimpses of her more tender parts are what drew me to her in the first place. I press my shoulders against the seat, rest my hands in my lap, and wait for her to continue.

"You're not dating Caroline anymore, right? That wasn't a dramatic embellishment in your monologue last night?"

The square inch where our knees touch feels like a conduit. I want to reach for her hands, but I tug my ear instead. "No, we really broke up. After you and I . . ." I feel my cheeks heat. "I couldn't think straight, and I knew it at least had a little bit to do with being in a relationship with someone I couldn't actually see myself with."

Marin nods. The train keeps rolling. It's almost as if I can see her stuffing her emotions down while her eyes trace the tree line out the window.

There's so much to say. *I think I'm in love with you.* Or, *I'm desperate to kiss you right now.* Or, *The dullest, bleakest phase of my adult life was when we didn't speak for years.* But instead, I just watch her. She glances at me, then back

EXIT LANE

out the window for the duration of the ride. It should be unnerving, but instead, a sense of peace floods my senses. It feels so easy to be around Marin. No one else—well, maybe Carter—makes me feel this all-consuming calm. I forgot about that part.

The walk to the Louisiana Museum of Modern Art from the train is dotted with charming houses and blanketed by wide-open sky. "Imagine living here," I say, then laugh when she responds, "I kind of do." Most of the day's crowds have headed back into the city by the time we check our coats, and we have entire exhibitions to ourselves. An Elmgreen & Dragset diving board, designed specifically for a windowed room, stops me in my tracks. The teal against the gray-blue that's darkening by the minute feels like an apt metaphor. I text Carter a picture with the caption "Here goes nothing," to which he responds, "Is this supposed to be a modern art meme?"

I watch strangers watch Marin. Maybe it's her ease that they notice, the way she carries herself with a sense that she belongs in every single room she steps into. It could be her height, which feels fitting amid the towering installations and the backdrop of evergreen pines. Watching her move, I try to dismiss the sharp pain in my stomach, a pain I've been carrying with me for months. It's a near-constant ache, right there, alongside joy and hope and what I'm starting to feel certain has to be love.

Marin and I barely speak, wandering from room to room, eventually finding ourselves facing the expanse of water separating us from Sweden. Arms crossed, she leans her head on my shoulder, and it's as if she's breaking the fourth wall between us. It's impossible to know what she's thinking. But this act of affection—this acknowledgment that there is intimacy between us—is enough at this moment.

"I don't know what to do with you, Teddy." Her voice is barely above a whisper, almost lost in the crashing of the waves. I wrap an arm around her shoulder, trying not to shake as we stand there, hopefully, on the precipice of something.

Back at the apartment, it's pitch black. Marin lights a sea of candles—"It's cultural. I'm not setting the mood"—and pulls ingredients from the refrigerator for chicken soup. She opens an ice-cold bottle of Grüner, which feels like the last thing I want to be drinking, until she lights a fireplace I barely noticed before.

"A real fireplace, huh? FourVC really hooked you up, Mar."

"And somehow, I still miss New York."

The pot's simmering in the kitchen now, and we're reaching our hands toward the warmth of the hearth. We keep finding reasons to stand closer together. The flames light her in amber. Kissing her is the only intelligible thought I can muster. She looks around the room, then back at me, straightening the collar on my sweatshirt.

The way she says "New York" makes it feel like she's

EXIT LANE

saying she misses me. I let my eyes drop to her long fingers wrapped around her wineglass, turning my shoulder into hers, and playfully reach for the drawstring on her cashmere sweatpants.

"I get the feeling New York misses you, too."

After dinner, dishes drying, we take the rest of the wine to the rug in front of the fireplace. She pulls pillows from the couch and sits cross-legged. Marin, the woman whose features I copy and paste on top of every other face I kiss, the person whose gestures I collect like seashells as she reveals more and more of herself to me, is laughing next to me, reaching for my knee to stabilize herself. Every micro contact turns me on, stirring a desire I swear has been dormant in every other romantic encounter of my life.

"But where's the slush? How does it stay so clean?" I ask. We're talking about snow in Copenhagen, but we're really talking about that night, when flakes were falling outside my window and we were in bed together with an ocean between us. Her hand stays on my knee, and her middle finger traces along the bone there. There's a gravitational pull tugging us toward the conversation. Momentum, wine, and the consuming effect of wanting this more than anything.

"New York is dirty," she says with a shrug. "That's part of its appeal." She sets her wine beside her.

We're going to talk about it. I inhale before diving in, hoping for the mentally clarifying benefits of oxygen, but instead finding the intoxicating scent of fireplace smoke and Marin.

"Everything you said that night," I start, leaning a

little closer, testing the waters, "is that how you talk to everyone on the phone past midnight?" Marin laughs. Our faces are closer than they've been since Envy's Pub. I could count the freckles on her nose if it wasn't for the cool darkness of this room, punctuated by the light of the fire and candles.

Her laugh now is not the one I hear most of the time. It's deeper, tugging at something she barely allows to see the light of day. I'm scared to move an inch, to break the spell of Marin unarmored.

"You know me, Teddy. I'm a phone sex addict with crippling insomnia." Her face grows pink from the middle, a softness washing across it. "That was my first time. I don't really know what came over me." Her flush suggests a bashfulness contradicted by her direct eye contact when she says it.

I reach for her forearm, reckless or jet-lagged or both. "Mine, too, but I hope you couldn't tell."

Her skin's soft, and I press my thumb against her pulse, wanting to feel her as much as she'll let me. If we kiss, it'll change everything, just the way it did the first time. There's nothing I want more. The seconds drag on while I wait for her to want the same.

Her conspiratorial smile, the way her collarbone moves with her breath against the button-down she's barely bothered to button. "I could tell," she says. "And that was part of the charm."

She reaches for my hand, tracing her finger over my pointer finger and thumb before resting her hand over mine.

EXIT LANE

The fire crackles. She shifts onto her hip, her eyelids drop, and then, like that, her lips are on mine, soft and deliberate. Every night I've wasted not on the phone with Marin, not here with Marin, unspools in one second—the moment she kisses me, five years later.

XV

MARIN

The kiss was bound to happen. I knew it the second I saw his face at my door. There was nothing in the cons column to stop it. Teddy makes me feel. It's that simple, and I hate that I want that despite myself. My typical rationales and the lengths I'll go to for self-preservation aren't worth anything with him. Even over the phone I felt helpless. Now, his mouth—his sweet, starving mouth—pressed against the corner of mine disarms whatever protective instincts remain. The only thought I have is *more*.

Teddy's hands are urgent. I'm somewhere between disbelief and delight, pulling my shirt off so I can feel closer to him. Every inch of my skin feels alive with sensation—the softness of the rug underneath us, the heat of the fire on my face, the wetness of our mouths moving against each other, the strain of my nipples against my bra. There's a current between us, bringing everything to the surface. I've felt this electricity before. But now there's a power supply fueled by years of unspoken conversations, thousands of text messages that were never sent, all the times our lives dropped us off at the other's proverbial front door. Then,

EXIT LANE

Teddy showed up at my actual one, and it feels shockingly simple.

He sighs when he sees me in my bra, the deepness of it a contrast to the shallowness of our breathing. "What is it, Teddy?" I tease. We can't stop kissing, not even when he lifts his sweatshirt and T-shirt over his head all at once. My lips, the cotton pulled over his lips, more kissing. Our bodies stretching and tangling into each other. This is the part where I normally start playing out the next twenty minutes, game-planning exactly what I've signed up for and preparing myself accordingly. But I can't get past his mouth, the way it falls on mine hungrily every time. His hand moves to the strap of my bra and gently tugs it down as his tongue presses deeper. I feel it in every part of my body, a throbbing between my legs, a magnetic impulse to be as close to him as possible. His other hand works its way into my hair, the soft part of his thumb presses against my ear. Nothing has ever felt so consuming.

I pull back, holding his face in my hands and watching him watch me, his eyes scanning incredulously, his need for me already obvious.

Unstoppable, that's how I feel.

Teddy hooks his arm around my waist, pulling me onto his lap, and I straddle him as he leans against the base of the sofa. Every muscle in my body softens to give way to the tension building between my legs. His hands run from my waist to my thighs, leaving a heat map in their wake. I'm caught between total surrender and wanting to memorize every moment. His cock pushes against his jeans and against me, and I feel desire everywhere. "Every time I look at you"—he kisses my neck, under my ear—"I want to tell you how desperately I want you." His teeth scrape at my shoulder. I reach around my back to undo my bra and then look down to track as his thumbs stroke my nipples. I shudder, feeling my stomach bowl out and my neck stretch in his direction. "I've never wanted to be your friend." He leans his head into me and kisses the words into my clavicle.

In one motion, Teddy stands with my legs still wrapped around his waist and carries me to my bedroom. The sight of him, arms flexed and chest flushed, is the in-the-flesh manifestation of every night I've imagined him while touching myself, the moments I've squeezed my eyes shut and writhed with enough fervor to conjure him in front of me. The real thing, it turns out, is even more compelling. "This is me," he says, his lips dragging across my neck, "asking if I can take off your pants. And your underwear." I can barely whimper a "yes." My head falls back against a mountain of sheets, and my heart starts racing as I watch him undress me. My hands reach for his waist, pulling myself into him, my need for him against his need for me. "The jeans have to go," I say, and I laugh as he undoes his belt and fights off his stiff denim with one hand, pulling my pants down with the other. This is the part I normally rush. With Teddy, I want everything to stay in slow motion.

He presses my shoulders against the bed, and I bask in the feeling of being fully naked in front of him. Almost on instinct, I move my hand between my legs, verifying that I

EXIT LANE

am as swollen and as wet as I feel. Teddy watches me, then gently grabs my wrist and brings my fingers to his mouth, sucking the taste of me off of them. "This is what I want," he mutters. "I've wanted this for so long, Mar. More than anything, I've wanted this." He moves my hand back to the pillow, pinning it above my head, and runs his tongue along the side of my neck. Then he's at my breasts, my rib cage, my hip, my thigh, leaving wet kisses and whispering my name with every exhale. By the time his tongue is dragging along my clit, his hands holding my legs open with authority, I am on the edge of release, my entire body electrified.

How many times in life is the real thing better than the hundreds of ways I imagined it beforehand? And why did I want so badly not to want this?

Steadying my hips, he looks up to see how needy I've become, and his attention on my face intensifies my desperation. "What do you want?"

"Teddy, I want you to fuck me," I manage between waves of almost orgasms. In this dim light, I can barely make out a smile before he plants his hands on either side of me and pulls himself up so our faces are an inch from each other. I pull his boxers down, and he kicks them off the rest of the way, landing them somewhere between my vintage armoire and stack of unread novels.

Our bodies together feel mesmerizing. I don't know how to get as close to him as I want to be—if that is even possible to achieve. As if he can hear my thoughts, he presses his chest into mine. I can feel his heart beating, and for the first time, I feel the thunderbolt of fear. This will be over. We'll have to put together the pieces of what's unfolding and make sense of what's next. With anyone else, this is when I start to make my exit plan, retreat into the recesses of my head to build up walls before anything can take root.

But before I can fall into old habits, Teddy loops an arm underneath me and rolls us over, flipping me on top of him. His palm is splayed against my lower back, and he pulls me into him. "Stay with me, baby," he says, reading my mind. Teddy's a flashlight on all my darkest parts.

So I do. I stay with him as he unrolls a condom I pull from my nightstand drawer. I stay with him as he pauses at my entrance, tormenting me as he takes his time teasing himself into me. I stay with him as he sinks into me fully, a groan escaping his lips, his eyes staying locked on mine. Having him inside of me feels like an untying of the knot that's tethered me to everything I've been afraid of. My eyes go wet, and I tilt my head back and rest my gaze on the ceiling. It's as though my whole understanding of my life and what I want from it rearranges itself around this moment in my bedroom.

"Tell me how it feels, Mar," he prods, bringing me back to the moment again, rocking into me and pressing the heel of his hand against my clit.

"Not like anything I've ever felt before," I respond, gasping, reaching for his head and holding it into my neck. No past, no future, no story. Just here. The naked honesty of my answer and the shifting angle of our bodies sends me over

EXIT LANE

the edge, and I can feel my walls convulsing and clenching around him. His release follows mine, one domino falling after the other.

I slip out of bed almost immediately after for the bathroom, and my rosy cheeks and knotted hair in the mirror strike me as a sharp contrast to my usual composure—more revealing than my actual nudity. I wait for a jolt of panic, but it doesn't come. "See what happens," I tell myself out loud as the water runs. I crawl back into bed, interlace my legs with his, and watch the silent snowfall out the window. As he kisses my neck and sighs into my chest, it's obvious neither of us wants to speak first. To start trying to make sense of what just happened. *I fucked Teddy McCarrel*, I think, leading with the facts. *And it was the best sex of my life.* This feels like the beginning of something monumental, terrifyingly so.

I decide to offer an out.

"We don't have to talk about it," I say. "This can just be something that happened when you randomly decided to visit me in Copenhagen if you want it to be."

Teddy's face drops, a flash of anger turning sweet, somewhere closer to conviction. "Mar, I'm sick of pretending like this isn't what it is. That it isn't exactly what I want it to be. I've never had sex like that before. I've never wanted to have sex with someone the way I've wanted to be with you all these years. But it's not about the sex—I mean, not that I'm anywhere close to processing that, but . . ." He reaches up and tucks my hair behind my ear, pulling his face to my neck.

"We're going to talk about this—ad nauseam. With breaks for more sex and more cardamom rolls."

A wave of relief. That my eject button was denied. "Whatever you say," I whisper, kissing him on the cheek and curling toward him.

"If that's you trying to ask to cuddle, permission granted."

Our exhales start to sync, and I struggle to keep my eyes open. "Can we do it all over again tomorrow?" His voice is small, tentative. All this time, I've been concerned with following a series of rules architected for control, too busy trying *not to feel* to give Teddy a chance. Too focused on racing off into all the tomorrows.

"I loved today." I kiss his jaw and smooth his coppery hair.

I let my eyelids fall, and as I do, I think about my dad, like I do most nights, and wonder what he would say. He and my mom were married at twenty-one with a reception in a church basement and pies baked by aunts on either side. "Love can be as complicated as you want it to be," he told me after he was diagnosed, the week I was waiting to be asked to homecoming by a now very happily out man who, at the time, I thought understood me like no one else.

"I didn't say anything about love, Dad, relax. I just want Dylan to want to be with me."

He laughed, leaning back against the front porch where we spent most nights after dinner. "Fine. *You* can make anything as complicated as you want it to be. The trick

EXIT LANE

is knowing what to let be uncomplicated." He died a few months later.

Teddy turns to his side, spooning me and snoring in my ear. I smile, wipe away a tear, and resolve to let this be uncomplicated.

XVI

TEDDY

The disbelief of waking up with Marin Voss's body next to mine jolts me. Last night replays in vignettes. Somehow it was everything I hoped and more than I expected at the same time. But that's her.

Amid the bliss, there's a tight pang of guilt. I know I have to deal with life, to return the voicemails from my doctor. *Do they leave you two messages if it's good news?* I wonder and pull the covers tighter. Right now, all I want is to stay in this hard-earned happiness forever.

"Hi," she whispers, rolling over toward me, the weight of her body bringing me back to earth. And back to wanting to forget it all to be with her. Her nipple peeks out from the sheet, and I cover it with my mouth.

We have the kind of sleepy sex I've always fantasized about—eyes closed, long kisses, sighing into each other's shoulders.

"I took the rest of the week off," she says, back from the kitchen with two cups of ginger tea. "And I promise I won't make us visit any more museums."

Instead, we spend the morning in bed, reading a pile

EXIT LANE

of *New Yorker*s she saved for an indeterminate future date and drinking cappuccinos. My phone dies on a counter in another room, and its existence barely crosses my mind. There are too many conversations to catch up on. We both try to read a book across from each other on the sofa but just end up making out. "You're very distracting," she laughs, tracing a finger along my jaw.

"We can read when we're dead," I respond, dropping to my knees before pulling her pajama pants off and leaning my face into the space between her legs.

We fuck in the afternoon and take a long walk for pastries.

Then we do the same thing the next day.

At night, I cook while Marin sits on the counter, feeding me bits of cheese and teasing me about all my Midwestern tendencies. "No, sweet Teddy, I cannot find you pepper jack, even if I agree it would be perfect on this."

Moving around the apartment, we stop to narrate the scene we're in, two people charmed by their own compatibility. "It's easy being around you. I've never felt that before." She's wiping off the counter and barely speaks above a whisper. "With everyone else, I feel like I have to be on or ready, but being with you feels like being alone, but better. I didn't know that was possible."

I wrap her in a hug and listen to her heart steady its beating. "I know exactly what you mean." And even in the silence, there's an invisible tin-can phone line stretching between us. I don't have to guess what she's thinking anymore.

Falling into a routine, our days eventually start to shift away from sex and popcorn in bed. Still, every quotidian moment—reaching for her hand at the crosswalk, watching her try on a gown for a gala next week, finding my favorite mug on her shelf—cements my sentiment that there's not a single person on the planet I'd rather do it all alongside.

I start running her a bath the minute she texts she's coming back from Pilates. She scratches the inside of my arm after we slip into velvet seats at the movie theater. I make a list of all the reasons why she should come back to Iowa with me, even for a weekend, and tape it to her fridge. She cries talking about how lonely it felt to become her sister's second parent when she was a teenager. I promise her I'll never ever leave, even though I'm getting on a plane in days and don't know what the future holds.

Before we're ready, it's our last day, and while she pops out for sustenance, I decide it's time: that I'd like to hear whatever medical update awaits while I'm still cocooned in this dream world with Marin. I step out onto the apartment's balcony to make the call, catching my doctor before he starts his appointments for the day. "We caught it early," he says as I grip the railing. "Rare for someone your age but very treatable," he continues as my eyes go searingly hot in the cold. As he transfers me to the receptionist to set an appointment for next week, the word "cancer" pings between every neuron in my brain.

When Marin returns, I'm slumped on the couch. I don't know how much time has passed. For a minute, I wonder if I should propose, before shoving the idea into the category of deeply irresponsible. I want to tell her my news as much as I don't want to tell her. I try to make my face neutral. I stand tall and hang up her coat.

"It's Tivoli," she says, craning her neck toward me in the entryway. "Our last night has to be at Tivoli Gardens." And what can I do but smile and kiss her on the top of her head?

When we arrive at the kind of amusement park reserved for picture books, the snow has painted it in an even more festive hue. The setting brightens each of the emotions swirling through me—tenderness, contentment, anger, fear—as they all battle to express themselves. My stomach grips like I've ridden the Fatamorgana looming overhead. Marin hands me a bag of warm, spiced nuts and a cup of hot cider when it hits me—the time-is-now gut punch.

MARIN

"Archery is over here. It's not real archery, so don't get too excited, but trust me, it's the best game on this side of the park." I tug Teddy's hand, but he stands resolutely under a weeping willow dressed in cascading Christmas lights. His eyes are wet, and his expression is strained.

"What is it?" My skin starts itching under my wool sweater, and I'm suddenly hot. The list of worst-case scenarios I kept at bay for the past week comes flooding in, knocking me backward. I'm still holding his fingers, but there's too much distance between our bodies. A space that now feels unnatural. I take a step closer to him, and my vision blurs around the edges, the sound of the park fading until I can only hear my voice, desperate, shaky.

"Teddy, I love you," I say, gripping him tighter. "I've been thinking about it all week, and I can say it now. I have no idea what it means—for us or for what happens next—but it's true. You're the best person in the entire world, and I have no idea why you picked me, but all I want is to figure out how to be as good to you as you are to me." I exhale, trying to smile, willing any powers that be to let us live in this moment under the willow tree for the rest of our lives. Teddy shakes his head, reaching for my elbows and attempting to steady both of us.

He's silent as tears start to fall from his eyes. Not the happy kind, not the emotionally-moved-by-the-monologue-I-just-gave kind. Children run screaming around us, but I barely hear them. "No, no, no," I whisper, eyes widening, willing this conversation in any other direction.

"I love you, Mar. Of course I love you. And I hate every single day we've spent not saying that to each other. I don't know about soulmates, not really, but if they're real, you're mine. If destiny is a thing we're lucky enough to hope for, it's what led me to you."

I hold his upper arms and kiss him, childishly thinking I can slow this whole thing down. *Every day*, I realize—I've thought about him every single day since we first met. And

EXIT LANE

I can't imagine going another day not telling him I love him. I say a silent prayer, uncertain to whom I'm making the request, for this to be the part where the tears are a good sign and nothing bad ever happens again.

"I have to tell you something." Teddy straightens up, taking a big exhale and folding his hands in front of him. I'm sweating through my mittens, and I stuff them into my purse, my eyes never leaving his.

"I'm sick." The world stops spinning for a moment. All the sights and sounds of Tivoli drop to a white noise. "I just found out today that it's cancer." He looks down. "But if I'm being honest, I think I knew in my gut before I came here that it was something. I didn't want to find out. I wanted to keep us safe by not knowing, and I wanted to protect you, Mar—you've already been through too much. But it's stage 1. And we're working on a plan."

That's what they said, my parents, the night in the living room when all four of us were huddled in a pile of tears and snot—the spelling list I was quizzing Violet on crumbled between the couch cushions: that they were working on a plan. There was never any plan. For my dad, it was always incurable, but for the next three months, I clung to that phrase, that ambiguous blueprint and its implications, like a prayer for a miracle.

"I'll probably have to take a medical leave from FourVC, but I'll know more next week. I love—"

I'm back at the family dinner table with my sister on my lap, the ice cream melting in our bowls, watching our dad break down in front of us. "It's going to be treatable.

It has to be treatable. We're going to get through this as a family, and I promise you, I'm going to be OK."

The fear shakes itself out of its dormant slumber. Teddy's different. I'm different. I'm not a child, and it's early stage, and he's going to be OK. But before I can metabolize any of this, before I can gather any rationality, I respond.

"How could you lie to me about this?" My voice is angrier than I want it to sound. "How could you keep this from me all week?" I wish I could hold him, promise him I'll be there for every appointment and take the best notes and send the email updates to our families and sleep next to him on the hospital bed. But I can feel the panic creeping up, wrapping itself around my lungs and my throat. For every part of me that knows this can be different, there are a thousand reasons why I'm afraid of it feeling like losing my dad all over again. Any empathy is overpowered by fear, which flips a switch somewhere inside of me.

"Sloane and Carter know?" The words come out three octaves higher than I mean them to. I don't know how I got them out at all.

He rocks his head back and forth. "That I was waiting on results—they know that. Not what the results are."

I count three breaths in for an inhale and three for an exhale. I can get through this. I can be strong for him. But then I think about those nights, alone in my bedroom, crying into my pillow, trying to make sense of the loss, and I am overcome with terror by the idea of going back there again. Something in me breaks, and the words are

EXIT LANE

out before I can stop them. "I can't do this again." Teddy pulls me in, arms tight around my shoulders.

I'm sobbing, shaking in his arms. *I can't do this?* God, what have I done? Deep in some cavity of my brain, I'm aghast at myself. But that disappointment is eclipsed by the need for this not to be happening, the instinct to protect myself from another loss I know I'm not strong enough to handle. All the memories of the past week, the certainty we felt, get shelved in the recesses of my psyche. The invisible thread between us is severed, like it was made of spider silk all along.

"You don't have to do anything." He's holding my shoulders, squeezing them, desperately searching for me in the vortex of all this. "Mar, nothing changes. I'm going to be OK." Hearing the line again, the one I carried in my pocket like a promise, ruins me. It wasn't true for my dad. It won't be true for Teddy. Grief is what I left in Iowa. It's the part of my story I outran and outworked, and I refuse to be pulled back into its bottomless despair. My resolution hardens as the rest of the park slowly comes back into view.

"I love you. And I can't go through this again. Teddy, I'm so sorry." I shove my keys into his hands and run, away from the cascading lights and into the dark night.

The frigid air cuts through my lungs, and I relish the pain. A hurt that can be remedied. I have nowhere to go—no plan—but my internal compass leads me to a cozy used bookstore a few blocks away where I once bought a gift for my mom's birthday.

The bell tolls as I duck in from the cold. The salesperson recognizes me and quickly grasps the state I'm in. "Love, why don't I show you back to the rare books room? Maybe some browsing and privacy will do you some good."

Among the dusty volumes wrapped in plastic, I drop to the floor and pull my knees close. Sobbing, I feel every ounce of regret for how I treated Teddy. It's the same flavor of regret I felt after seeing him drive away when he dropped me off at my first New York apartment and after hailing a cab from karaoke, but there's a sinking feeling that accompanies the sharpness. Like there's poison on the blade. I register it as a self-inflicted wound: The pain I'm feeling now is just as excruciating as the sadness I'm trying so desperately to protect myself from.

It's not too late, I tell myself. I could run back to the park, take it all back, and love him through this terrible thing. But instead, I sit, paralyzed, for an hour while the tears fall.

I make it back to my apartment in a haze, and when I do, his stuff's cleared out and a note sits on my nightstand. "I love you. No matter what. xTMc."

There's nothing to do but call Sloane, who answers on the first ring. "Hi. I know. You don't have to explain. Carter filled me in. I wish I was with you right now."

I start sobbing all over again as I wrap myself in the sheets that still smell like Teddy. "Oh, M. Just put me on speakerphone, and we can talk when you're ready."

XVII

TEDDY

At the airport, I shut myself into a bathroom stall so I can cry and call Carter before boarding the flight I rebooked on the way here. "I'll meet you in New York. We'll do this together." It's simple when he says it, like getting an MRI scan to rule out any other tumors is what every guy in his late twenties does when he's overdue for a catch-up with his best friend.

The flight feels eternal, the liminal space offering an unwelcome home for every doubt and fear. The scene of Marin and me at Tivoli plays out in slow motion, on repeat. Our time in Copenhagen, entrapped as if in a snow globe, always felt destined to shatter. I know better than to think things could be as simple forever as they were for one perfect week. But the back-to-back blows I've been dealt today are made all the more painful by the sense that I should have seen them both coming. "Devastated" isn't a big enough word.

Maybe I can win her back, I think. *After I'm healthy*. My face crumples, and I turn toward the plane window to hide it as I'm struck with the heart-shattering reality: She doesn't love me enough to go through this alongside me. Mar loves me when it's convenient, those nights she's alone in a new city or needs a ride or wants to be reminded of the life she'll never let herself return to. Hope fades into something closer to resentment, but not enough to stop me from scrolling through the dozens of photos I took of us on my phone until the pilot announces our landing.

Carter's there, waiting at the gate, a suitcase of his own in one hand and a posterboard scrawled with "It's going to be OK" in the other. "Sloane's made you watch too many rom-coms, man." I laugh for the first time since getting the news and pull him in for a hug.

He squeezes me tighter. "I figured if I put it on a fucking sign, maybe we'd find it easier to believe."

At first, with the constant beeping of machinery as my only consistent companion, Marin is the lone thing on my mind. I must waste hundreds of hospital cafeteria napkins penning letters to her I never send. Their content ranges from "I'm sorry" to "How could you?" before circling back to "I miss you."

The true road to recovery starts with an all-beige short-term rental apartment in Rochester, Minnesota. Dr. Ng thinks keeping a degree of normalcy, a.k.a. my own toaster oven, will be important to the success of the treatment. Basking in my autonomy, trying to ignore the couple across the hall scream-fighting at six in the morning, I butter some

EXIT LANE

sourdough before heading in for a regular appointment. I'm at Mayo Clinic most days, and when I'm not, I'm here.

My entire life has shrunk down in size. Even the heartbreak, which seemed to take residence in every crevice of my brain, has contracted over the month I've been here. I think about Marin when I'm falling asleep, longing mixing with anger, sadness with grief, and I imagine her here. Not because it feels realistic. But because the thought of it brings me back to my happiest self, before any of this seemed real.

I was ready to let my love for her dictate the rest of my life. I turn the thought over and over one night while falling asleep, practically marveling at it. In the hours I've spent staring off into space under an IV, I've considered every possible excuse for her reaction. None of them pass inspection. She forced my hand. Moving forward can't involve her. What's next has to be with someone new, someone who loves me—even when it terrifies them.

I have grand visions of keeping my life—my real life—on ice through my treatment, but after going back and forth over email with the Head of People at FourVC, that bubble bursts. I can take twelve weeks of medical leave, but their policy doesn't leave room for working from Minnesota. They offer to pay for weekly first-class flights to and from the city and hint at a substantial severance package as the alternative.

It's obvious this is the moment to use the emergency fund I've been saving for almost a decade. They'll extend my health insurance through the end of the following year, and getting better can be my only focus. I don't know that

I want to hear from Marin, but this makes it all the more likely that I won't.

During the second month of treatment, everything starts to shift into some kind of new normal, in the way that life does. Carter flies up every other weekend. My mom and dad stay in the spare bedroom when they can, or my sister does, visiting from the University of Wisconsin. We play board games on Friday nights and try not to talk about upcoming scans. They all know I'm contending with something emotionally beyond this disease, but they don't ask me to share. I take great Midwestern comfort in their avoidance.

MARIN

Violet and Sloane visit for spring break, and I plan an entirely new itinerary for their week with me, eliminating any stops that I test-drove with Teddy. I keep us impossibly, exhaustingly busy, nervous that any downtime will invite conversation about what happened. I plead with Violet to regale us with tales of undergrad antics and pepper Sloane with questions about the upcoming table read for the screenplay she finally finished. I never once bring up my own emotional turmoil. I don't tell them that for the first time since the months that followed my dad dying, I wake up in the middle of every night drenched in cold sweat and unable to fall back asleep.

Dropping them off at the airport, I give Violet a Rolex

EXIT LANE

watch, a smaller version of the one of my dad's that I wear every day, as a graduation gift. "He would be so proud of you, V. I'm so proud of you."

She pulls me in for a hug, one that says what we can't, and when we step apart, she looks at Sloane, giving her the kind of sisterly nod that turns my stomach into an instant knot.

Sloane sighs, reaching a hand out for mine, but before she can make contact, I cross my arms.

"I'm sorry. About Teddy." She forces eye contact. "It's a really hard time for all of us, and I know you don't want to talk about it, but I also know you're not OK. I can't—we can't leave here without at least acknowledging it."

I look away, toward the security line. We were so close to never addressing it, even if the tension was palpable every second of their visit.

"Sloane, I can't—" I sigh, frustration overtaking me. I pull my mints from my bag. "Violet, head to your gate, OK? You don't have to hear this, and you're boarding soon anyway."

I'm shocked to see Violet widen her stance, feet planted on the printed carpet. "You broke his heart, Mar." Her indignant tone matches Sloane's. "He's sick. I don't understand how you could do that."

My eyes dart between both pairs of theirs, searching for something to anchor me. "I . . . I . . . losing Dad almost killed me. I still carry it with me constantly, and it fills every crevice in my life that I don't find a way to fill with something else. I would do anything to avoid the hurt of that loss, and I have spent every day since trying to get further from it. I can't . . . I can't go through that again. Not for Teddy, not for anyone."

Sloane starts crying, quietly, her body pitching against Violet's for support. "He's not *anyone*. Teddy is the love of your life, and that is so fucking obvious to everyone around you, and you'll never get to know what that feels like as long as you're scared to let anything happen beyond your control. I love you. You're my best friend. You know that. But I'm so disappointed in you."

We stand in stunned silence as they wait for me to respond. When I don't, Sloane kisses me on the cheek, then rests her palm on my jaw and locks eyes with mine like she's trying to impart wisdom, strength, or both, before walking Violet to her gate.

Home, alone, without the warmth of playing slumber party with Sloane and Violet or the bliss of playing house with Teddy, my apartment feels pointless. What's the meaning of all these artisanal dishes sitting empty in the cabinets? These beautiful throws I just want to hide under?

I distract myself with tidying, listening to "Nothing Compares 2 U" on repeat until the Bridget Jones vibes become too unbearable.

Changing my sheets, I notice one of Teddy's threadbare Iowa T-shirts smashed between the mattress and the headboard. The realization starts as a question, seeking any

EXIT LANE

chink in the armor of my self-protection. *What if Sloane was right?* What if the person who makes me forget that time exists, the person who has cataloged every single one of my emotions by how they present on my face, the person who shatters me with a single glance, is my way out of this hurt? And what if the thing keeping me in this despair is me?

Maybe protecting myself from more heartbreak and any future grief is as pointless as pretending bad things don't happen. Folding the T-shirt, holding it against my chest, I let the revelation wash over me. I've made a horrible mistake that I'll never come back from, not as long as I care about Teddy enough to hope he can find the selfless partner he deserves. I picture him in a hospital bed, and I don't see my dad or think of myself. I imagine being with him for this impossible, terrifying next thing. The idea of him facing those endless appointments and complicated decisions and me being here sends me into a fresh bout of tears. That I ruined any chance of that.

I wash three sets of espresso cups, three forks, and three plates in the sink, aware of my loneliness, and commit to at least making amends with everyone I've been pushing away. I write Sloane an apology email without proofreading it. I leave Violet a voicemail telling her I'm going to start back up with therapy and saying sorry for not sharing what I've been going through. For not being the sister she actually deserves by being one who opens up to her the way she does to me.

I call my mom. It's been weeks since we last talked, and I'm nervous as the line rings. "Hello, Marin?" Just the sound of her voice undoes me. "Mom," I whimper, curling into a corner. "I messed up."

I haven't come to her with a problem since middle school. I always told myself it was because I didn't want to give her anything else to deal with while I watched her buckle under the weight of her own grief, but I wonder if it might be because I didn't want to need her. Didn't want to rely on a parent when I knew how abruptly they could be ripped away.

She listens as I sob into the phone, and she repeats that it's going to be OK over and over again. After a few minutes, I steady myself enough to ask if she knew my dad was the one, a conversation I've always meant to have with her. "From the minute I saw him, doing donuts in his car in the snowy parking lot." Her voice takes on a softer tone, the nostalgia making the conversation between us more tender than usual. "And it terrified me at first, loving someone so much." I wait, catching my breath from the crying. "I waited for it to dissolve. But that fear, that never really went away. I just carried it with the love, and I still do, with you and Violet."

She sends me to bed with the promise to call the next day—"just a quick hi, so I know you're still with us"—and I hang up feeling if not better, exactly, then not entirely hopeless.

The next morning, I put off catching up on work and start drafting Teddy a letter. I'm rewriting it for the ninth time

EXIT LANE

over lunch when I see Carter's name flashing on my phone. I feel stuck on an inhale.

"Is he OK?" I answer. My relationship with Carter has always been mediated through Sloane, our shared connection with Teddy rarely acknowledged.

Carter clears his throat. I start pacing. We've never spoken on the phone before, and the unfamiliarity of it puts me even more on edge. "He will be. Marin, it's a lot, everything with Teddy, and I wanted to ask you for something, and I know it's awkward and probably doesn't seem like my place, but it is my place because he's my best friend, and—" Carter pauses, stumbling over his words, and I am desperate for him to just spit it out. My mind is spinning with the possibilities of what he's going to ask. Does Teddy need money? An organ?

"If you were thinking about it at all, and I don't know if you were, but either way . . . please don't reach out to him. Please let him heal on his own. You almost broke him in Copenhagen, and he needs every ounce of strength he can muster right now."

All the regret and sadness I've been carrying throughout my body consolidates in a tight ball at the pit of my stomach.

"I know that . . . and I know how selfish I was. And I want to apologize to him."

"He doesn't want that right now."

"He doesn't want that, or you don't?"

"He doesn't." Carter clears his throat again. "He told me." A deep shame washes over me. I respond immediately.

143

"Of course, Carter. I'm so sorry." I start sobbing, the irreparable damage I've done setting in, and I don't try to hide it.

Carter softens. "Mar, Sloane will make sure you hear if anything . . . big happens with him. We know you love him."

I gasp for air. "Just please take care of him."

I hang up without saying goodbye and force myself into the shower. As if I can pretend the tears aren't pouring out of me if there's water flowing over me too.

Wrapped in a robe, I turn back to my computer to delete the email I've been drafting to Teddy, but even I have to acknowledge that the level of emotion I've laid bare in text is something of a personal first. Instead of erasing it, I reach for a little hand-painted notebook I bought when I took Sloane and Violet to Etiket. Cracking it open, I copy down every word, if only so I can have a record of how it feels to love someone like this.

THREE YEARS LATER

XVIII

MARIN

As I dig through my tote for my notebook, the leather of my bag slouching in the space between my personal pod and that of my neighboring passenger, I realize how long it's been since I've been back to Iowa. I go to New York for work almost every month—for board meetings and partner meetings, business trips enhanced by dinner with Violet or one of her PR events and the occasional tried-and-true hookup. At thirty, it's harder to get excited about the potential of encountering a perfect new person and a lot easier to send an Uber to bring Gabby from her place in Williamsburg to my favorite room at the Marlton. "Move back," she whispers as I go down on her.

But my life in Copenhagen is easier, and I like that about it, something I can't bring myself to admit out loud. A lack of close friendships leaves time for me to have hobbies, something my life in New York never seemed to allow for. I take morning barre classes and plant herbs in my kitchen. I see my therapist every Wednesday and started riding horses outside the city most Sundays.

My evenings are my own, which usually means tackling an ever-growing pile of self-help books and prompted journals. I've even started working toward building my own investment fund—something my stability-loving self would have shuddered at the thought of a year ago.

A late-night film or a walk around a well-lit park, they're mine if I want them. Plus, there are plenty of fucked-up workaholics to date in Denmark, too. Instead of telling Gabby any of this, I make her come, kiss her shoulder, and assure her it's my job that's keeping me away.

In three years of visits back to the city, I've yet to run into Teddy. There are eight million people there, but our nonencounter still feels improbable given our track record. His existence is like a shadow in my life. Part of his charm has always been his lack of online presence, and I do my best not to pester Sloane with questions. I've heard that his treatment went well, and I know that I hurt him too much to deserve any more information than that.

But Sloane and I are still Sloane and I. When she and Carter FaceTimed me with a diamond pressed to the front-facing camera, I couldn't have been happier, or less surprised. I'd been emailing with Carter about Sloane's ring for almost a year. "And the best part"—Sloane sighed, smiling at Carter before looking at me over the phone—"is that we're doing the wedding in Iowa City. Iowa Shitty, Mar! It deserves to be immortalized."

As maid of honor, I've gone all out at every opportunity. A long bachelorette weekend in a cottage in the Cotswolds with a male dancer wearing only an apron while serving us

EXIT LANE

high tea? A smash hit. A bridal luncheon for Carter's and Sloane's extremely buttoned-up moms at Mayflower Inn? One for the books. Dress shopping, which mostly entailed a forty-three-part email chain between me and Sloane? Weirdly emotional. But I've learned enough about myself over these last few years to know I'm overcompensating for fear that I'm not going to be able to pull off what lies ahead. It's Iowa I'm worried about.

It's the turn off the interstate where my dad is buried, which used to just be the exit we'd take to get BBQ after church most Sundays. It's his best friend's house, the place we thought of as a second home, where I haven't been since he's been gone. It's the basketball court in the backyard of our old house, where we'd shoot free throws for hours until my mom turned on the back porch light. "You can't control anything in life," he used to say, switching out our regular ball for the late-night version that glowed in the dark, "except your free throws."

Shifting in my seat, I try to read one of the *New Yorker*s I packed. The wedding's on Saturday, send-off brunch on Sunday, best friend debrief session Monday before Sloane and Carter jet off to Antigua. I'm cutting it a little close flying in on Friday afternoon, but I couldn't bring myself to book anything earlier. I'll make it there right before the rehearsal dinner, slip into a silky matching set and loafers, and charm the pants off of the aunts and uncles I haven't seen since our graduation.

Last night, packing with Violet on FaceTime, I asked her to weigh in on jewelry options. "Won't Teddy be there?"

she inquired gingerly. I suppressed the part of me that believes my job as her big sister is to convince her my life is stable, settled, and safe.

I'd realized I'd been holding my breath and exhaled. "I mean, of course. He's Carter's best friend." Even through an iPhone screen, I could tell she was searching for something in my eyes. "It'll be good to see him again. I think it'll be reassuring to see for myself how he's doing."

Ever since my screwup, I've been collecting dispatches to Teddy in the same painted notebook where I transcribed the email draft that Carter intercepted when he called. Some nights, I write to him about the horrible dates I find myself on with towering Danish men who insist on pulling out my chair when we sit for dinner. Other times, I write a list of questions about his treatment, about where he's living, basic pleas to color in his distanced life. After too much wine, the notes lean wistful and saccharine, my longing for him evident in every sentence I scrawl. The letters are mostly a reminder of how much I miss him and how one-sided that feeling has become. Last night, after zipping my suitcase shut, I wrote a short missive. "I'll see you tomorrow. I'm so terrified you hate me. Please forgive me. Please hug me and tell me you're doing OK and that we'll both be OK somehow." The whole notebook reads like this—cheesy, unedited, but honest. Sharing my thoughts with this clutch of paper makes me feel less alone with them, and I've come to count on its proximity.

"We'll be landing at Chicago O'Hare Airport in forty minutes," announces the pilot. "We're experiencing some snow, so bear with us on what might be a bit of

EXIT LANE

a bumpy landing. Seat belts fastened, please." The eight hours evaporated with me lost in my own thoughts, and I suddenly want more time to prepare or distract myself or otherwise avoid what comes next.

Landing feels precarious as the plane seems to slip, just slightly, as we taxi to our terminal. As soon as I hear the ding, I pull down my suitcase, nod to the flight attendant, and make my way to my connecting flight.

I step off the jet bridge, and my palms start to sweat, even before I notice the crowds huddled around flight information displays. More flashing red text populates the screens by the minute. Weaving past customer service lines, I hurry to my gate, hopeful the forty-five-minute connection to Iowa City is local enough to be unaffected by the snow accumulating outside the airport windows.

Even here, in my long alpaca coat and cashmere sweater, I can sense the brutal Midwestern wind. I check my watch, trying to calculate the hours I have to get into my silk suit. Approaching my gate, I see it's full, thank God, but as I get closer, I start to worry the mass might not be a good sign. "We're offering reimbursement for a local hotel and booking on the earliest flight out tomorrow," mumbles the agent.

I stop short, and my forehead tightens. "No, no, this isn't happening," I mutter to myself, incredulous at my stupidity for scheduling the latest possible travel, as if I hadn't grown up with this weather. I steady my hand against a charging station, trying to push past jet lag and into problem-solving mode. I'm getting to Iowa City. I just need to figure out how. But before I can consider a plan, I see him.

XIX

TEDDY

I never imagined a sense of dread would accompany a trip to Iowa, but I've been fighting nerves since I booked my travel, the latest itinerary I could manage. This is supposed to be the place I can always come back to, but it feels like something else right now, a series of unwelcome reminders and realities. Marin and everything she represents, the well-meaning questions I'll field about my health from people who know me only as the Promising Young Man Who Battled Cancer, my parents placed in a setting that reminds me of the cracks in their own union.

And that's just the twitchiness I feel before rumblings of incoming weather from the flight crew somewhere over Ohio fix me to the edge of my seat.

When we land, I notice flashing cancellation signs out of the corner of my eye and the snow falling out the windows. A winter wonderland in other circumstances, a hurdle to overcome in this one.

Approaching my gate, a message over the loudspeaker confirms my fears: Flights are grounded. Someone is yelling at the ticket agent. Someone else is slumped against a concrete wall, coat tugged over their head. And then there's a tall woman with an intense stare and a hand tucking her hair behind her ear. There's Marin. The only other person in the world who'd cut it this close on her flight home. The person I think of every time it snows.

I hate how much better the sight of her, the certainty of her, makes me feel. That, against all odds, she is still a comfort to me as we stand amid crowds of tense passengers in an airport while the likelihood of us being with our best friends to celebrate one of the most important moments of their lives decreases exponentially. That she's still ethereally beautiful to me straight off a transatlantic flight with a scowl on her face. And then she sees me. And the corners of her mouth quirk up.

MARIN

I don't know how Teddy manages to show up at just the right time, every single time, but he does. It's been three years. That's hundreds of times I wanted to call him, a couple of dozen I've masturbated thinking of him. I can sense my face flushing. It's the kind of feeling that renders me immobile.

The old Teddy would have run over with a wide smile plastered on his perfect face, pulled me in tight, and said something like "Mar. Of course you're on the last-minute flight." But present-day Teddy has every reason in the world to keep his distance. And his apprehensive expression says as much.

There might be a thousand different ways to play this: pretend I didn't spot him, beg for forgiveness on my knees on the patterned carpet, respectfully wave from afar. Something deep within me takes over, and I'm suddenly in motion, walking toward him. His surprised expression says I didn't do what we both probably expected: run in the opposite direction.

I try to make out every detail of his physical well-being as the distance between us disappears. He's a little slimmer than in Copenhagen, when he lifted me onto the counter with one arm around my waist. His hair is cropped closer, less boyish. His posture is stiffer, like when I first met him. Like the ease he'd found when we were together was temporary too.

"Hey," I offer, unsure where else to start. It's clear from the way he barely turns his body toward mine that this is going poorly already.

"Really? Three years, and that's your best line?"

I have so many lines, I think, *and I don't know if I have the right to say any of them.* But here and now, it can't be about us. "Can we figure out how we're getting to Iowa City, and then we can talk?"

He must hear the pain in my voice because he nods, almost imperceptibly, and bites his lip. When he finally turns to me, the sight of him makes my breath lodge in my throat. Blueish-purple bags under his eyes and thinner eyebrows than I remember. Quiet reminders of all he's faced over the past few years. An ambush of guilt for every single day I wasn't by his side.

EXIT LANE

Teddy points me to the unruly customer service line. "This is your penance. I'll go try to rent us a car. Keep me posted."

Alone in a mob of angry Midwesterners, I try to catch my breath. "No flights out of O'Hare means no flights out of O'Hare, folks," shouts an impassioned customer service rep over the din.

There he goes, the one that got away, on his way to rent us whatever vehicle, ideally with four-wheel drive, is left. The rehearsal dinner starts in hours, but it's hard to remember it's my primary concern. To think past Teddy's lips, the suitcase he's carrying that I last saw on my bedroom floor, the way he keeps moving forward somehow and all the ways I've let him down by being stuck in my past.

My phone vibrates from my coat pocket, and I realize a half hour has passed and I've moved up three feet. On my screen, a photo of Teddy and me kissing that he must have set as his contact when he was in Copenhagen—the two of us rosy-cheeked walking home with cardamom buns. My eyes prick, and I press at them with the heel of my hand. He's calling me. Something that I never thought would happen again.

"Hi, yes, hi," I struggle to answer.

"Meet me at rentals. Spot H31."

I find him in the parking garage with crossed arms and the satisfied smirk he gets when he pulls something off. I take anything other than a grimace as a win. "Options were extremely limited," he starts, popping the trunk on a traffic-light-yellow BMW hatchback. "I had to beg the rental guy to give me anything at all. He seemed to think it's too dangerous to be on the road, but I assured him I'm a very careful driver."

"When's the last time you took a road trip?"

"Not sure the ATVs at Carter's bachelor party count as a road trip. Maybe not since we did Iowa to New York. As I'm sure you'll recall, I got both of us there in one piece."

Yes, it's me that broke us. I duck my head and pull my coat tighter.

Sliding into the passenger seat, our initial encounter floods back to me. The silence of the broken radio. His arm propped up against the window in a way that made me notice muscles I'd never bothered to see before. That jukebox. That kiss.

"We have to call Cart and Sloane," he says, pulling his phone out of his pocket.

"Absolutely not, Teddy. They're getting married. They don't care about our canceled flight. I'll text Violet, and she'll take care of it." It's the most myself I've been with him since we spotted each other.

He tilts his head, and my heart races. He drops his phone in the cup holder, and my gaze falls to his hand. *It's just a hand*, I chastise myself. *A mere appendage.* But my head swims with memories of those hands on me, the way he pressed them against my breasts, how he dragged them across my hip bones, opening me up before making me come. His hands circling my wrists above my head while he stared down at me. His hands tilting my chin up to kiss him while he was on top of me, both of us lost in

EXIT LANE

those seconds before orgasm when our brains emptied of everything but a single syllable: you.

"Do you mind? Pulling up directions?" he asks, clearly not for the first time.

I shift my focus to my own phone. Our drive to Iowa City should only take three hours on a normal day, but the sheet of snow outside the parking garage predicts we'll be lucky to get there in six. Turning out of the airport, Teddy wipes his palms on his wool overcoat.

"We'll take our time," I say. He nods and looks straight ahead.

We merge onto the interstate in slow motion, careful to avoid the snowbanks newly formed on medians and the other cars whose forms we can barely make out.

"Can you tell I'm nervous?" His blinker has been on for the last minute, and we're going roughly eighteen miles per hour.

"Yes," I whisper, "but so am I."

XX

TEDDY

There's something eerie and comforting at the same time about being one of the only cars on the interstate. Semi-trucks sit lined up at gas stations, waiting out the storm, through snow that shows no signs of letting up.

Marin's quiet. I'm glad. I focus on the road in front of us and any still-visible markers that might help me stay on it.

After Copenhagen, there was a part of me—the part that put Marin at the end of every best-case scenario—that couldn't go on. Getting better was for me, for my parents, for Romy, for Carter, and for a hypothetical someone who would stand by me through remission. Getting better meant letting go of every version of my future that included Marin. I couldn't believe how many iterations—us in Denmark, in New York, in Iowa—I was willing to consider for her. And yet her imagination couldn't stretch past me being sick.

It was easier to dismiss her as callous and detached when we weren't just a center console apart. Being near her reminds me of both the reasons I held a candle for her for so long and why I extinguished it with such

EXIT LANE

force. Her stupefying blend of tough and tender, inscrutable and obvious, impenetrable and open. The astonishingly high standards and steadfast rules she clings to, for better and for worse. The deeply tender and bruised heart at the center of it all.

She's had a terrified expression plastered on her face since the moment she spotted me at the gate, but underneath the weight of it, I sense a spark—the same rush I feel at being in each other's presence again.

The last time I felt this confounded by her presence was on this same stretch of highway. We're right back where we started, and I still have no idea where this will go.

"Do you want to just listen to music for a little while?" I offer an olive branch, hoping to avoid conversation, anything real. *I knew Marin would be here*, I remind myself. I just thought we'd nod at each other during the rehearsal and maybe smile for some pictures as we bookended our best friends.

"Yeah. Yes." Marin connects her phone to Bluetooth. "I'll let you know when we need to exit, but we have a while."

I listen for a sign in every song she plays, something like a cosmic arrow pointed in the direction of what's next. Could the Prince acoustic cover be a callback to our night at Sing Sing? Does the Sufjan Stevens song allude to something beyond the state we're in? She sits with one leg crossed over the other, leaning into the space between the door and the seat, as beautiful as ever. She pulls the hair that falls in front of her face behind her head, twirling it into an impossible bun that just as quickly slips apart. I want to tell her how angry I've been. To tell her how I've considered every possible explanation for how she acted and none of them have been good enough. To express how utterly infuriating it is that the most highly capable person I've ever known gave up on something so easily because it was hard. I want to ask her everything. I want to obey the ever-expanding part of me that aches to give her another chance. But instead, I keep driving.

The car moves at glacial speed, the steering wheel tugging as the tires meet patches of ice. Pickup truck wheels laced in spikes plow past us. Every minute the GPS puts us closer to Iowa City is a relief. Who plans a winter wedding in the Midwest? People who insist on getting married on the anniversary of their first official date, I guess. People like Sloane.

I let the sliver of my brain not laser-focused on driving drift to Carter's cousin Lucy, my potential wedding-weekend setup. She's a Dartmouth grad with a high-profile job in DC working for Teresa Powell. The highlight reel Carter presented me included accounts of how she swims laps every single morning and sweeps at poker nights on the weekends. When I received a text from an unknown number on my way to the airport that read "Looking forward to meeting you x," I felt relief knowing that no matter our chemistry, I'd at least have something—someone—else to focus on aside from the person who broke my heart weeks before I started chemo.

Maybe I could build a life with Lucy, have two and a

EXIT LANE

half kids and move next to Carter and Sloane and store Christmas decorations in giant plastic bins in the garage and host annual Fourth of July parties. Lucy could be the thing I've never found in New York. Lucy could be the thing Marin never could be.

"You're daydreaming. Snap out of it. Focus on the road."

But there she is. She's harsh and hilarious. She's bracing—a shock to my system. And still, after all these years, even when I'm swirling with sadness and anger, it feels like a rare and special privilege to get to be alone with her.

Her dad's death hardened the outside parts of her, but those mornings in Copenhagen, I swear I'd never seen someone so caring and vulnerable—so open to the possibility of love. But then she threw it away—every single memory we built together disposed of so she could cling to her fear. Her inability to be with me through the toughest years of my life.

"Did they tell you I'm the best man?" The words are out of my mouth before I've thought them through. *Why are you doing this? Giving her an opening?* I berate myself.

She looks up, her eyes—ten shades bluer than I remember—fixed on mine, stirring the same feelings in me they used to.

"Of course they didn't tell me. Sloane and Cart love to use the phrase 'separation of church and state' when the conversation comes within ten feet of the topic of you. Which, to be clear, is not the right usage of the phrase. They never talk to me about you."

161

"Same. Once, Sloane let it slip that you were seeing Gabby when you were in New York and immediately followed up with an apology email."

"Well, I'm not *seeing* Gabby, first of all. We just hang out when I'm in the city for work. And what I'd accept is an apology email for the timing of this marriage ceremony."

I laugh, and the sound mixes with the intro of a Kenny Loggins classic, either an act of fate or the Spotify algorithm screwing with us. Shoving my resentment and hurt aside, I speak for the piece of me that always hoped I'd be able to talk to Marin again.

"You never tell me when you're in the city," I say, voice low. I squeeze the steering wheel tighter.

She shifts in her seat, like she's adjusting to the sea change, first furrowing her brow in defensiveness, then stifling a pleased smile and tossing her phone in her bag.

"For all I know, you're married in Copenhagen with a kid and a dog." Before she can respond, I continue. "Which is a joke, obviously, because you're committed to a life devoid of joy, and you hate pets."

She laughs, a real Marin laugh. "First of all, I'm only ever in for a couple of days, just enough time for work, dinner with Violet—she lives there now—and occasionally a nostalgia fuck." She blushes as we both sit with those words—that Marin could ever be nostalgic and that I could never be just a fuck.

The sound of Kenny Loggins's vibrato echoes. Just the mention of sex sends a slideshow of our greatest hits to

EXIT LANE

the front of my mind. I try to ignore the image of Marin arching her body on top of me, fresh out of the shower, my hands anchoring her thighs.

"Second, I've been given explicit instructions never to reach out to you again. You could be the one with a dog and a wife for all I know." Her tone softens at the end as we both realize how little information about the other we've survived off of for the past three years. How much we've been feeding off of crumbs.

I refuse to read into her mention of instructions—the notion she might have behaved differently if permitted otherwise—and press on. "My Hinge profile's hard at work: Single. Open to something casual or long-term. Votes Democrat; leans disillusioned. Drinks in a way that's not a problem. Has both an income and a savings account." And because I can't resist, or maybe because I feel the karmic imbalance of letting her off easy, I add, "But Carter has promised me an introduction to a very promising cousin of his, so the story could be different after tomorrow night on that portable dance floor."

"Lucy's cute, but she only goes for old-money guys. Hate to break it to you." Marin delivers her verdict without pause as she slips her arms out of her coat, leaving it draped over her shoulders. "Plus, Sloane and I are like 90 percent sure she's a lesbian. But maybe you have a type?"

She looks up, her expression some uncanny mixture of smirking and pleading. Kenny Loggins is belting out the bridge, and I see the Marin I miss more than anything. Behind her jabs, there's everything else that's ever been expressed between us. Our eyes lock, and I feel her starting to say things I'm not sure I'm ready for.

I wipe a palm on my pants, sweating for a million reasons, when I spot hazards blinking. As I edge the car to the left out of caution, the median appears more quickly than I anticipate. I overcorrect, feel the wheel slip out from under me as we hit a patch of black ice and spin into the ditch. Neither of us scream, all of it happening in hyperspeed, and the stereo keeps playing over our racing hearts.

XXI

MARIN

Stuck somewhere in a snowbank on the side of I-88, our hatchback settles at an angle as we catch our breath. "Are you OK?" I ask, reaching across the console to check for Teddy's seat belt before he can respond.

"God, yes, I'm fine. I just sort of hit my head on the headrest, but I'm OK. Are you OK?"

His hand reaches for mine, and the touch of his cold fingers is steadying for the split second before we realize we've made contact and return our limbs to our respective halves of the car.

I scan my body, like I'm doing a guided meditation, grateful for every inch unscathed. Then I catapult into fix-it mode, transform into Work Marin. How can we get from A to B most efficiently?

"We need to get the car out of here before any more snow falls."

Teddy nods. His relief when I take over is palpable. When I turn to look at him, really look at him, I see that his hand is shaking, but his breath is slowing. I can feel my brow crease, and I'm flooded with the desire to take care

165

of him. To demonstrate that I can. "We'd be very stupid to get back on the interstate at this point. We'll pull off and check in to whatever hotel is closest. I'll just keep checking the weather so we can leave the second the snow stops."

Teddy runs his fingers through his hair, laughing to himself. "Funny how you're great in a crisis as long as it's not personal."

"I'm sorry, Teddy. Did you say something?" I shoot back. Like I wasn't just having the same thought.

"Just remarking on how you can get us out of a literal ditch but broke up with me because I told you I had cancer. That's all." His tone's cutting. Even though I know I deserve it, the sentence slices.

As if on cue, a towering pickup truck whose bed is bigger than the room I rented when I moved to New York pulls up to us, blinding us with its headlights. The matte black finish rules out the possibility of law enforcement. Without a chance to check the bumper for right-wing political sentiments, I'm paralyzed, but I try to be optimistic at this turn of events. At the very least, I'm grateful for the large-scale distraction from the conversation I'd like to put off as long as possible.

The headlights dim. A silhouette capped by a cowboy hat makes its way to the driver's side door.

"Haven't we been through enough today?" Teddy sighs.

"I'm handling this." I move closer to him, and my core clenches involuntarily.

The figure motions for us to open the window, and Teddy closes his eyes and grits his teeth as he does. The

EXIT LANE

frigid outdoors spills into the car, along with a considerable amount of snow.

"Y'all need a tow?" the mysterious shadow yells, his profile aglow in the car lights. Two perfectly plucked brows and an orange paisley button-down under a full-length down parka greet us with a beaming smile. "Watched you spin out and thought I'd see what I can do. If you're keen, I can get you hooked up and on the road in a minute or two."

Relief and a renewed faith in the universe wash over me. Teddy looks like he might cry, so before we can all bear witness to male fragility, I lean over him and respond. "That would mean the world to us. Here, I can pay you?"

The Danish krone and pile of five-dollar bills I pull out of my monogrammed wallet makes our hero laugh. "Doesn't count as an act of kindness if you're compensated, now does it? Stay put, and when I honk, you hit the gas as hard as you can."

He disappears back into his pickup to string an impressive setup between our two vehicles.

"What?" I roll my eyes at Teddy. "I'm not going to question it. I'm just going to accept it as some sign from the universe and go along for the ride." Heat radiates off of him, and I wonder if our somehow-minor accident unlocked a well of rage. "What other option do we have?"

I retreat to my seat and buckle back in. Our unfinished conversation looms between us. But getting out of a ditch tops getting closure from a breakup on Maslow's hierarchy. As promised, we hear a honk, and Teddy leans on the gas.

Snow flies out from under the back tires, but in an instant, we're back on the road, like we never left it in the first place.

Our friend comes to say goodbye, and now Teddy's regained his composure enough to thank him politely and profusely.

He brushes us off. "You were stuck, and I could help. You two make a great couple, by the way. I'm always offering to help people get their cars unstuck—part of the fun of driving a pickup. So many of the couples I come across are fighting and screaming too loud to hear me honk the horn to drive."

We smile politely, and I grab Teddy's hand. "I'm lucky. I mean, we're both lucky." There's no reason for me to convince this stranger that we're actually together, but the opportunity to touch Teddy and act like it's all for the bit wins out. Teddy's glare softens, which makes me wonder if maybe he doesn't mind—if I still have the ability to charm him, whether he likes it or not.

With a tip of his hat and a wave, our savior is back in the cab of his truck. As he pulls away, I watch "Follow me to the gay bar" and "Honk if you're letting the soft animal of your body love what it loves" bumper stickers recede into the distance. "We were visited by an angel," I whisper as I reach for my phone, desperate to find a place to sleep, get some food, and have my ass handed to me for the biggest mistake of my life.

EXIT LANE

TEDDY

I should be thinking about where we'll spend the night, how we'll get to Iowa City, and all the apologies I want from the former love of my life for the hundreds of ways she let me down.

But while Marin's fixing things from the passenger seat and I'm driving ten miles an hour in the right lane, I find myself wondering, for the first time, what forgiveness would look like. It's been three years of promising myself to never let Marin back in, trusting that there was nothing to resurrect. But all it's taken is a few hours back in the car with her for me to start questioning everything all over. I know I'm not the same person who stood under the willow at Tivoli, but is she? I guess the worst that can happen is she breaks my heart. And I've survived that and cancer already.

Marin laughs, and it's louder and higher than the sound I know. "You're not going to believe this," she says with her hand over her mouth. "I swear this is the closest option. Pinky promise it is." She reaches to loop her little finger into mine on the steering wheel, and it's one of those moments of tenderness I know I'll replay over and over. Her guard slips for a split second, and she's just a person delighted by the odds that dropped us in this snowstorm in the first place.

"Exit here, then turn right."

As I coax the steering wheel, I feel anticipation laced with dread. *It can't be*, I think.

But then, like a switch has been flipped, the unease

dissipates. All of me, every cell, hopes my guess is right, and as I pull past a row of trees, there it is. Envy's Pub—aglow in the snow, a warm beacon of nostalgia and excellent bar food and full bottles of Ranch dressing. "No fucking way," I whisper.

We're out of the car in a daze, and when we cross the threshold of the bar, it's as if we've been gone for hours, not years. Pockets of people nod in our direction, raising beers in what feels like a hometown welcome. "Shut the damn door!" someone yells, and my heart warms.

"I just love being back in the Midwest," Marin whispers and winks, taking my coat from my shoulders and hanging both of ours up in a makeshift closet next to the jukebox.

"Two whiskeys on the rocks, please. And chicken fingers and mozzarella sticks," she says to a bartender, a different one from last time but somehow the same. Settling onto a barstool, Marin looks ten years younger. Her eyes flash to the jukebox—like it's her mark, identified for later, once we have a plan.

I pout over to my seat next to her, loving and hating that I feel like a puzzle piece fitting into place. "This is . . . how are we here again?"

She stands out in a cashmere sweater and aviator reading glasses she pulled somewhere from her bag. I want to make the case that I could pass as a local in a sweatshirt and jeans, but I have to admit that we're both giving City Folk. That, this many years removed from cornfields, we're even less likely patrons than we were on our first visit.

"We're here because it's too dangerous to drive, so we

EXIT LANE

need to wait it out. The fact that it's the same bar, that's just . . . well, I don't know what that is, Teddy." She takes a healthy sip from her whiskey, her profile in this light revealing bags under her eyes I didn't notice before. "Don't even tell me what time it is in Copenhagen." She smiles.

Someone puts "Hotel California" on the jukebox, and before I have a chance to conjure a reaction, she rests her face in her hands, elbows on the bar, at the exact moment our food arrives. "Jesus Christ," she whispers with a rueful chuckle. "The only remedy is fried cheese."

I clear my throat, uncertain of what I really want to say but starting to feel like we're past the point of avoidance.

Marin lifts a hand. "Let me go first, please." She shifts in her seat. "I fucked up in the most unforgivable, selfish way. I think about the ten thousand other ways I could have responded to you that day constantly. I was scared—of how much I loved you and how real losing you felt. But none of that's an excuse. I was the meanest, cruelest person to you that day. I don't deserve the chance to even tell you this, but that's the grace of a wedding weekend in a snowstorm I guess." She exhales, taking a quick sip, and before I can respond, she goes on. "You are the best person, Teddy. You have somehow made me—*me*—feel like people are pre-destined for each other in some cosmic way. And I ruined that. So go ahead, lay into me. I promise the small fortune I've spent on 'healing modalities' has prepared me for this exact moment."

"I . . . I don't know what to say, Mar." Five hours ago, I could have unrolled a scroll of all the reasons why she

171

was correct about being the worst and would have kindly asked for this to be our last conversation. But then there's her—real, in front of me, asking for forgiveness in a way that pulls at every part of me that believes in reconciliation, in second chances. I speak before I can process what I'm saying or what the consequences might be. "I forgive you. Of course I do. You hurt me so much, and I thought I might never be able to, but eventually I did forgive you. Because despite every effort you've made to be unknowable, I do know you. And I know what part of you won out in that moment. And I care about you too much to let either of us stay stuck there. I forgave you long before I stopped resenting you, which, for the record, may have only happened in the last hour or so. If it's happened yet." I watch her face soften, watch fear transform into familiarity.

"Friends," she says, scooting her barstool closer to mine. "For real this time." She stretches out her hand for me to shake, and I picture it wrapped around a karaoke mic, a bag of pastries, the curve of my jaw. When our palms meet, the stomach drop her touch brings registers as a shock even though I knew it was coming.

XXII

MARIN

We're splitting a cigarette in the cold, one pilfered from a local insurance agent who tossed us a matchbox printed with his face. "Perfect execution." Teddy laughs, examining the man's likeness on the cardboard and lighting the Camel dangling from my mouth, inches from his.

Our conversation went better than I expected, which is to say, we're not screaming or crying in the blustery parking lot. But instead of feeling the relief of a resolution, I'm somehow even more on edge. Teddy's perpetual kindness sets my head spinning, and I try not to let my hope spin out of control. The mere promise of the situation warms my body, inching me closer to where he leans on the building's facade.

"Sloane's calling," he says, motioning for me to lean in to answer. The screen's bright between us, his hand shielding it from the snow, our red noses almost touching. Drunk and blissed out at the roaring success of the opera flash mob at the rehearsal dinner, she's taking our absence in stride. "Are you kidding? How could I be mad? It's so filmic." I roll my eyes, smiling. "I'm just thrilled you two haven't jumped each other in a bar fight yet. The fact that you're standing close enough to take this call is good enough for me."

Our lack of distance hits both of us at the same time. Teddy's hand has been casually resting on my shoulder, but now it darts into his pocket.

Sloane isn't done. "You know you both did this to yourselves by taking the last possible flights. I've done enough damage control for you two over the years to know why. Go to bed. Leave as soon as the roads clear. I can't wait to kiss you both." We hang up, laughing, and head back into the bar.

Nursing a club soda from our seats, I watch Teddy across the room as he reenacts the black ice scene for a group of truck drivers who are just as surprised about our miraculous pickup salvation as we are. He's beautiful, more beautiful than all the times I tried to conjure him after he left. The way he speaks reflects light onto the faces of everyone in conversation with him. These men are glowing, the subject of his total attention. When he turns to me, waving me over, I catch one of the truckers remarking, "I'm just saying, if she's not yours, I'd like to take a swing if you know what I mean."

"I can't shake this one, unfortunately for you. She's like my shadow." He playfully tugs me to him by my waist as I make my way to the jukebox, silently grateful to not have to fend off rounds of drinks from the increasingly male population at Envy's.

This act he's putting on is a joke. It's a ruse. But the simple idea of being his anything makes me blush. Our

EXIT LANE

eyes keep finding each other when they don't need to, when I don't mean for them to. I turn away from the group to queue up "I Feel for You" and then "Borderline" and, because I owe it to him, "Hotel California."

Back on my stool next to him, I barely listen to the conversation he's found himself locked into about weight limits and traffic cameras. His new friends have migrated to the bar with us. Picking at the fried pickles we must have ordered at some point, I note an overwhelming sense of peace in his proximity. Absentmindedly, if there is such a thing, he lets a hand rest on my thigh, moving his thumb slowly back and forth over the inseam of my jeans. The friction sends a current between my legs. I move my hand, which was propped on the edge of his stool to stabilize me, to reach for the belt loop in the back of his jeans. *How did I ever think straight when he was touching me?* I wonder.

"We're on the way to our best friends' wedding," he says, smiling at me, mischief in his eyes where there was hurt only a few hours ago.

"Maybe you're next?" The group lifts their beers in our honor while Teddy presses his forehead against mine as our glasses clink.

"I should be so lucky," he whispers, only loud enough for me to hear. I want all of this to be real, bankable, the kind of fortune you read about in epics. As heat spreads across my entire body, I accept that my promise of friendship hours ago was once again a lie.

When I hear the opening synthesizer of "I Feel for You," I wait for Teddy's reaction. He turns to me and grabs my shoulders with the same urgency he brings to everything he's excited about. At this point, our stools are practically overlapping, and our legs haven't stopped finding reasons to knock into each other.

"Did you know that Prince played all twenty-seven instruments used on his 1978 debut album *For You*?" He kisses me on the cheek, like it's the most natural thing in the world.

And for a moment, it is. The two of us, together, reminds me of everything I ruined.

"Brilliant." I drape my arm over his shoulder, blinking my eyes furiously and pushing away all the things I want to profess, all the ways I swear I'll do better. Instead, I lean against him, giving into the warmth of his orbit and the unlikely way I respond to the worn-in and safe home I find there. He leans back.

Carter and Sloane send selfies with "Big kiss x" as the caption in a group chat that's been dormant for years. I send back a picture of Teddy dancing under a hot dog topping menu. Quarters from God knows where keep appearing. Leaning against the glass of the jukebox, Teddy tugs at the sleeve of my sweater, sending shivers across my arms.

"Pick something good." He tilts his head against mine. "You're my fake girlfriend, and I've elected myself as mayor of this bar."

"I saw. Interesting technique."

"You charmed your trucker on the side of the highway, and now I've charmed mine." He steps closer, closing the neon glow from the jukebox between us. "But really. Pick

EXIT LANE

something good. I make it a habit not to date women with bad taste."

Instead of bringing up the time he told me about Caroline dragging him to a Tiësto rave, I put on Sheryl Crow and try to calm the butterflies that seem to have taken up permanent residency in my stomach.

An hour later, we're splitting a hot dog with "all the toppings," which turns out to be a thing people say in movies and should never mean in real life. Relish and sweet pickles topple out as we hover over a plate splattered with mustard, ketchup, and mayo.

"Delicious," Teddy says, swallowing and throwing his head back before lifting the latest addition to our bar-food sampler toward me. As I take a bite, I catch the tip of his finger in my mouth. A blush spreads across his cheeks, and my entire body warms.

"It's time to play a game." I clap my hands once. I'm clear-eyed, two giant glasses of water in my system and enough sleep deprivation to know exactly what I want. "The game we played on our road trip."

"Let's go back and forth and tell each other what we know to be true about the other person," he recites back to me, both mocking and wistful. "God, Mar. You scared me so much, and I thought you were so fucking cool." Our smiles are inches away from each other, every instinct in my body instructing me to slide past pragmatism straight into pleasure.

"I'll start," I whisper, his hand on my thigh, my heart beating louder than I knew it could.

XXIII

TEDDY

"The first thing I know about you is that you have every right to hate me. And I am prepared to spend the rest of my life regretting how I acted. So the fact that we're here," she motions dramatically around us and smiles, "feels like a second chance I don't deserve."

All the dozens of ways I imagined this conversation taking place over the years—in my apartment in Minnesota, in the hospital waiting room at Mayo, in the Brooklyn Heights studio I rented when I moved back to New York—and I could never have pictured this. Marin's eyes try to find a clue in mine, any indication that what she's saying is landing. All those appointments alone, wishing I could send her darkly funny cancer memes or complain about the endless blood tests—they added up.

I let my knee rest against hers. "I did hate you. And then I missed you. But then I hated myself for missing you." I pause, cautiously approaching wherever we're headed next. "You didn't know how to show up for me. It didn't matter how badly I wanted to believe it was a traumatic situation for you and that given another chance you'd never react the

EXIT LANE

same way. I had to make peace with the version of our story that broke my heart: When I needed you to care, when I needed you to roll up your sleeves and figure all this out next to me, you left." I pause, giving myself a moment before saying the thing I've never let myself dwell on. "It made me feel like maybe I wasn't worth caring about or caring for, Mar, and that made me hate myself. That's why I had to shut you out completely."

Marin stares at me with a look of shock on her face, her eyes watering. She covers her mouth with one hand and starts digging through her purse with the other, desperate to find something. She pulls out a pocket-sized notebook with worn corners and gives me the kind of pinched look a kid gets when they're explaining their artwork to the class. Tears are running down her cheeks now, and I can feel the urgency and remorse before she even speaks. "At first, I drafted you an email. But then when Carter told me not to contact you . . ." She places the notebook in my hands. "I started writing to you here—when I was waiting for a meeting, after a bad night out." Flipping through the pages, I see dates from the past three years accompanied by passages in Marin's impossible-to-decipher cursive. "It's all the things that reminded me of you. And all the ways I wanted to say I was sorry. How I envisioned our life could have been if I hadn't fucked it all up."

I realize the hand I meant to playfully rest on her thigh hasn't moved. A heat stirs in the center of my stomach. I want to talk about our feelings, and I want to play this stupid game because I'll do whatever it takes to be near her.

But really, what I want is to move that hand from her thigh to in between her legs, drag it over the seam of her jeans and then under her shirt up her stomach, over her breasts, around to her back, and under her waistband to reach the spot where her ass curves into her eternal legs. I want to show her how much my body missed her body.

It's terrifying to have the thing I told myself would never happen, not in a million years, unfold in front of me. Part of me is holding back, expecting her to run at any moment. But most of me wants to embrace this improbable present, throw everything at it.

I grab her hand without overthinking it, watching her Rolex catch the light, taking in the beauty of something as simple as her fingers. "This scares me, Mar. Shitless, if I'm being totally honest. I had to get pretty comfortable with the idea of a future without you."

She pulls her hand from mine and rests her palms on my thighs, leaning close enough to my face for me to count her freckles. "If you want me to disappear back into my life in Copenhagen, I'll do it. No questions asked." I watch her carefully consider what she's about to say, her usual armor fading into something softer, more vulnerable, just as freaked out as I'm feeling. "But if there's a part of you, like there's a part of me, that wants to do this, really do this . . . to be together, I'm yours."

I can't begin to process what I've just heard. That everything I wanted three years ago is right in front of me.

Marin slips the notebook back into her bag, wiping the tears from her face and straightening her posture.

EXIT LANE

I wait for my thoughts to organize themselves like they normally do, but my mind is like an abstract painting—broad, messy strokes of shock and sorrow, longing and heartache, desire and horniness, trepidation and terror, all bleeding into one another. This is a person I felt resigned to hate. Who shows up for me only in the most outlandish of circumstances but not in the moments that make up my actual life.

She reaches for my forearms, a desperate joy washing across her face. "Teddy, things are different now. We're here, again. We can start over. I can do better."

"Things are different now for you," I respond without thinking. "It doesn't get to be that simple for you, Mar. You don't get to dip out for the really fucking hard part and then show up when everything's OK. When I'm healthy." Before I can soften the blow, "Last call!" rings from the other side of the bar, and we're snapped back to reality without warning.

I put a few hundreds on the counter without another word to her and shake hands with our server, who insists on giving me a hug. Marin watches stonily, handing me my coat in silence and pushing the door open, forcing us out into the cold.

The snow is softer now, spiraling as it falls. "You're best to stay put for the night," says a friendly trucker we threw darts with as he hoists himself into his cab. "But you two lovebirds won't mind." We drag our suitcases through inches of snow to the familiar motel next door. I wonder if Marin can hear my heart beating through my chest or sense the swirling confusion behind the cheeky smile I give our friend as he waves good night. I wonder if she can hear me trying to convince myself that she doesn't just want me because it could be easy again.

Inside the lobby, the air's stale, and we're greeted with a grunt from the woman behind the counter. "Hi." Marin strains for a name tag. "Hi, Dolores. We're stuck on our way to our best friends' wedding and hoping we can rent two of your finest rooms for the evening."

It's funny to watch Marin try to be charming, because she is, when she's not thinking about it. Dolores grimaces as Marin sets her visibly expensive bag on the dusty counter covered in local business cards.

"You think you're the only two stranded tonight? I don't have any rooms left."

Marin turns to me, eyes wide and desperate for help. Her natural response would likely involve a hasty bribe, perhaps a threat related to the Better Business Bureau. It's on me to bring a little Midwestern softness to the situation at hand.

"Hey there, hi, sorry for the night you must be having. Apologies for making yet another ask of you. We're happy to take anything you have. A janitor's closet. A laundry room." And in a moment of East Coast elitism, I pull out three remaining hundred-dollar bills to sweeten the deal. A polite, considered bribe.

Turns out, Dolores speaks the universal language of cash. "There's one room. 831. It's small. The hot water doesn't reach. Be out by ten." I could kiss this grumpy

EXIT LANE

receptionist. I reach for Marin's suitcase and tug our luggage down the hall.

"Nice move, Teddy. Very well played." I can't tell if Marin's poking fun or is as unnerved by our double-occupancy predicament as I am. "Who needs hot water anyway?"

XXIV

MARIN

"So it's not the Four Seasons," I quip nervously, spreading a towel across the desk before unpacking my toiletries, "but it's also not a semireclined passenger seat in a snowstorm."

My plan is to try to get to bed, lights off, as quickly as possible. The longer I'm awake, the more I will have to metabolize the last few hours, which I'm not prepared to do. Teddy's reaction to my bid for a second chance at the bar stung, especially painful because I deserved it. I've given him the impression I think I can just waltz back into his life. It's killing me that I don't know how to demonstrate, in some meaningful, convincing way, the truth: That what I did to him at Tivoli is not who I am. That I would never do that to him again. That we are this close to the Iowa border and all the emotional baggage and uncertainty that it carries, and yet my conviction about him is stronger than ever.

Teddy steps into the bathroom, and I look around the room. I avoid dwelling on the lack of a pullout sofa—or any furniture beyond a dresser and bed—as I focus on locating my decidedly unsexy gingham pajama set from my suitcase. Teddy starts brushing his teeth, door open, and I wince at

EXIT LANE

how familiar the sound is, still. Any chance I had at winning him back, proving to him I've changed, feels bleak at this point, and I don't want to think about it again until the storm passes. *He's better, and we're on speaking terms,* I remind myself. That alone is a better outcome than I could have hoped for.

"I'd offer to sleep on the floor," he calls out over the running water, "but I'm pretty sure there's concrete under this carpeting."

As soon as we were assigned this lone room, I knew we'd be sharing a bed. Actually agreeing to it is something else altogether.

I have to make light of it—have to play the part of brusque Marin who is unbothered by the presence of this man. It's my only defense. "Don't worry. I'll control myself despite the irresistible allure of your cotton boxers from college."

I blush as I say it, thankful he can't see me, and I think about the nights in Copenhagen where we'd go hours without clothes, one of us tiptoeing into the kitchen wrapped in a quilt to make tea. The time I ran out for wine in my giant parka and only a bra and underwear beneath because I knew I'd strip down as soon as I returned anyway.

I step up to the sink with my own toothbrush, desperately aware of how comfortable it feels to be lost in a quotidian moment next to him. This is what I missed most when I thought of him—sex, yes, a thousand times, but the quiet peace of being in his orbit. He slips out of the bathroom, pulling off his shirt and folding his pants the way he does every night. "Don't fuck this up," I mouth to myself in the mirror, desperate to get out of my own head. I brush my hair with the same brush I use every night, my heart pounding. I examine myself in the mirror, the bags under my eyes a little more pronounced. I reach for the cream I almost never use but pack anyway. I look for excuses to dawdle.

"You going to sleep in there?" Teddy asks from the bedroom with just enough teasing in his tone to tell me the chilliness of our Envy's Pub exit has thawed. I've extended my skincare routine well past its typical five minutes. Anxious, I click the light off, feeling my way toward the bed. As I tentatively pat at the mattress, I meet only a sheet. We're both partial to the side farthest from the door.

"You took the bad side," I say.

"When Dolores comes for you, she'll have to get through me first."

It's quiet as I climb in beside him. As my eyes adjust to the light, I can tell he's propped up on his elbows, and I can fill in the rest of his shape from memory. "Look, Mar, we both need to go to sleep. But I just wanted to say . . ." He sighs. "We can talk about this more tomorrow." Sleep. My body is intensely aware of its proximity to his. I can't imagine my heart rate slowing and can only hope that the jet lag, whiskey, and sustained fight-or-flight hormones will catch up with me.

Teddy reaches across the bed, and I hold my breath. He flips my collar right side out. "I'm donating this to a good cause," he says, tucking his only pillow perpendicular to mine, remembering my preference to curl into something, usually his chest, when sleeping. Lumpy barrier between us, I swear the tug between my body and his will keep me up all night. That's the last thought I have before I fall asleep, Teddy next to me.

XXV

TEDDY

Here's my definition of bliss: waking up to Marin's warm body curled against mine, her hair a thousand different directions, and a puddle of her drool collected on my sleeve. This is an enduring personal truth I can't deny even if it's a complicated one.

The bedside clock is flashing 7:21, and I ease out of the sheets to check the snowfall through the window. There's a sea of white, but nothing is falling from the sky. We're going to make it to Iowa City on time. The solace that brings last seconds. It's almost immediately replaced by nerves about what happens next.

Tiptoeing back to bed, I spot the notebook she pulled out at the bar peeking from her bag. It's not snooping if the entire thing is addressed to me, right? If she put it in my hands and encouraged me to page through it the night before? I reach for it. I extract it gingerly and crawl back beneath the covers, careful not to wake Marin.

On the front page, dated almost three years back, I read the first entry. "Teddy, you're at Mayo, getting better, and I'm here, in Copenhagen, wishing more than anything I could be with you—wishing I hadn't ruined that for both of us."

The entries vary from there, one a diagram of her new fund's thesis, another a list of birthday gift ideas she had for me but would never be able to execute. Flipping at random, tears fill my eyes, and I land on a list of everything she'd tell her dad about me if she could. "You're the exact kind of person he asked me to hold out for when I was twelve and grossed out by the idea of kissing anyone. You two have the same annoying trait of knowing what I need that I won't admit that I need." I turn to watch her, chest rising and falling, and feel the warmth of all the things she could never say but, turns out, could write down. The regret and hope she'd clung to these last three years.

I land on a note from nine months ago. "Sloane and Carter called to tell me they're getting married, and I couldn't be happier for them," it starts. "But when I got off the phone with them, I cried. I'm jealous that they both have what it takes to make this commitment to each other work when I failed you so completely. All my life, since I was fifteen, I have been looking for escape routes to get further and further away from my past. To carry myself far enough afield that maybe I wouldn't even be able to find my way back if I wanted to. But being with you—it was like finding the exit lane that would take me back to myself. Being with you showed me that I could be who I am now and who I was then, and that made me feel more whole than I had since my dad has been gone. Even if we never speak again, you will have forever changed me."

EXIT LANE

My eyes are too bleary to keep reading, and a tear falls on the page. "Mar," I whisper, unable to stand another minute without her. "Marin." I smooth her hair behind her ear. As her lids blink open, she jolts up to sitting, confused, before softening her face toward me. For a second, I think we might kiss. I'm done wasting time. Grabbing her hand, I press the little notebook onto her chest.

"I read it. I probably should have asked, but I figured if it was for me . . . Marin, I'm, uh . . ." She pushes the hair out of her face and opens her mouth to say something, but I continue. "I didn't know. For the last three years, I didn't know what you were thinking or feeling, but now I do. You love me, and that scares you. You can be scared if you want to be, but I'm not."

Marin's face twists, and I watch in awe as something, guilt or relief, works its way through her body. Then, without warning, she starts crying. Sobbing. "I don't want to be scared with anyone else." She gasps, her tears running onto my bare shoulder, our bodies pressed against each other as my own tears start to fall.

"You're the love of my life. I think you know that," I whisper into her ear, running my fingers through her hair.

MARIN

The notebook. The notebook I couldn't leave the house without for fear I'd have something I needed to tell Teddy and wouldn't have a way to say it. The pages I filled with ramblings of how I could work remotely from Iowa and how we could build a guest room for our siblings and host cornhole tournaments with Carter and Sloane. On one of the last pages, on the plane, I drew a map of Iowa City and the spots there that now made me think of him, even though we'd never been there together. "Everything reminds me of you," I wrote, resigned to Teddy's hold on all the places that matter to me for the rest of my life.

But here he is, at a roadside inn somewhere in Illinois, one hand cupping my jaw and the other reaching for my top button.

We kiss like we're breathing, like it's the most natural thing in the world, like survival. He pulls the small of my back closer to him, reaching beneath my pajama shirt, sending the same message to my brain I get every time we touch: Why haven't we been doing this forever? Teddy sighs as he kisses my neck, his erection pronounced against my thigh. No amount of fantasizing could prepare me for the very real, very desperate need surging between the two of us right now.

I peel off my top, and his mouth moves from my neck to my breasts, teeth clamping down gently on my nipples. Never in my life has sex felt so present. Like there is nothing else in the world, not even the room we're in. Every inch of my body and brain are lit up in Teddy's touch. I sit, straddling him, and drop my head to trail my tongue along his chest and his abs. Watching him watch me, I pull his boxers off, move down his body, and wrap my hand

EXIT LANE

around his dick, leaning down to lick before taking him in my mouth. "You," he whispers. "This."

His fingers twirl through my hair, and I close my eyes, focusing on the presence of his body. The muscles where his hip meets his stomach tensing under my palm. My mouth glides up and down him as he trembles, the press of his dick against the back of my throat and the groan it elicits each time it makes contact. Being able to give him pleasure like this turns me on so much I start to writhe against his leg, desperate for friction between my own.

"Marin," he pants, his fingers gripping my shoulder as my mouth fills with the taste of him. He is still for a moment, head back and breathing heavy, but then in one swift and decisive motion, he pulls me up so we are face-to-face and starts kissing me forcefully. His hand moves between my legs, his fingers spreading me open before he puts two of them inside of me. "I missed this so much," he whispers into my mouth. "All of this." His thumb presses firmly against my clit as he says it, and the pressure is too much, everywhere, all at once. As my orgasm crests, so do my tears.

XXVI

TEDDY

Marin's body softens against mine in a pile of scratchy sheets and sweat. The morning light illuminates the room, covering our naked bodies. "Why did we go three years without that?" I mutter, tracing my fingers across her back, taking in every detail of her form.

She rolls over and takes my face in her hands. "That's on me." Marin wraps the top sheet around herself and walks to the window, pulling back the curtain tentatively.

"My love," I say, the words comforting in my mouth. "This is the Midwest. I promise you, they're not going to let snow sit on the interstate overnight. The roads will be fine."

She scampers across the room like it's Christmas morning, tripping over her makeshift sheet dress, and kisses me on the cheek. Every second we spend like this feels dreamlike, nearly inconceivable. I can't help but romanticize the winter storm that landed us here as I listen to the plow trucks back out of the parking lot.

"I'm going to try to channel cold-plunge energy in this shower," she says, then pauses, puts her hand up. "But not, like, in a wellness way. In a we-have-no-other-option way."

EXIT LANE

At that, she drops the sheet and crosses into the bathroom. My eyes trace down her neck, her back, her legs. These parts of her I'll get to see and touch and kiss again and again. A marvel.

I check my phone. Two texts from Carter. A few from my parents, and a message from Violet. "Sorry if it's weird I'm texting you, but Mar's location is somewhere in Illinois, and she won't call me back. I think she's with you, which makes me feel better. Will you just let me know when you can?" I smile at the screen. I assure everyone that we're in one piece and on our way to Iowa City. "More soon," I type.

Marin dresses in silence. I let myself obsess over the way she wraps her bra around her rib cage, feel the way my heart drops when she asks me to button the back of her shirt. I don't have to collect these moments like they're scraps. I'm so used to being starved of them that I don't know how to respond to the abundance.

"Here's what we're going to do," I say as I repack the trunk of our rental that seems somehow even more yellow in the light of day. "We'll stick to the interstate, take it slow, and focus on finding a real espresso option as soon as possible."

Marin laughs, leaning in to kiss my cheek, her giant sunglasses pressed against my face. "I love letting you make the plan."

On the road, snow mirrors the late-morning sun back at us. Crosby, Stills, Nash & Young plays on the radio. A little Stevie Wonder. It takes herculean focus to steer the hatchback within the plowed lines and not reach over to hold her hand.

"Being in the car with you still makes me nervous," she jokes. The GPS says we're an hour and a half out.

MARIN

Sitting in the passenger seat just a few miles into Iowa, I wait for my chest to clench the way it always does when I enter this fraught territory. But as we pass the signs to Davenport, my breathing stays steady, my shoulders are relaxed, and I still have a smile on my face that I don't hold back. It's like I've broken a spell, and there's nothing left to feel but hope.

Teddy reaches for my hand, pulling it in for a kiss, his eyes never leaving the road. "You're it, Marin Voss—worth every single night I fell asleep missing you." We grip each other's fingers too tightly, a physical expression of the emotions we've been clinging to separately for too long.

Snow starts falling, but not like before. Instead, it's a dusting of individual snowflakes spinning before they land.

I owe it to Teddy to prove what I wrote in my notebook is real, to show him that it's not a diary: It's a record of my real feelings and real intentions, ones meant for him to hear. I need to say the words I wrote to him out loud while he's actually here in front of me, where he can hold me accountable.

I press my back against the door and turn my body to

EXIT LANE

face him, pulling my leg onto the seat. "Teddy, I *could* be in Iowa with you."

He grins. "Well, good thing, because you *are* in Iowa with me. Right now."

"No, Teddy." I reach across the console and rest my fingers on his sleeve. "I could live in Iowa with you."

He glances over at me just long enough to gauge that I'm serious, then puts on his turn signal.

He pulls over to the shoulder of the road, puts the car in park, and unbuckles his seat belt at the same time. He twists toward me and presses his mouth against mine, a perfect fit of two uncontrollable smiles.

And then he laughs against my lips. "Marin," he says, holding my face in his hands, cold from the steering wheel. "You are not moving to Iowa. That coat," he gestures at the plush fabric draped over my shoulders, "does not translate in Iowa."

My smile falls, and he kisses my forehead, then my brow.

"But I'm not moving to Iowa either. It turns out, against all odds, and maybe even against my will, I am a New Yorker. Or at least I am for now." He runs a hand through his hair, coppery in the sun. "That thing you wrote in your notebook about Sloane and Cart's wedding, about connecting the different parts of yourself . . . you changed me too. In order to make it through the last few years, I had to orient myself toward the future—fearlessly—and I learned that from you."

I hold his wool lapels and kiss the tiredness under his eyes. I look up at him. "So no Fifty-First Street, then?"

He laughs. "Not anytime soon."

"Would you accept, at the very least, me moving back to this continent? To be with you?"

He's silent for a beat.

"I would love that." He tucks my hair behind my ear and leans into me so our foreheads are touching and our eyes are locked. "I want you to do that."

When he pulls away, I can see our breath in the cold. He turns back to the wheel and starts the engine, then rests his hand on my thigh. "Ready?" he asks, and I nod.

I lean toward him to put my head against his shoulder, and we pull onto the highway. I check my map. "Fifty miles from where it all started."

"Yes," he says with a smirk. "Fifty miles and eight years."

Continue the trip with Marin and Teddy: Read the book's epilogue, stream their playlist, wear Teddy's perfect rugby tee, and get Marin's made-in-Iowa notebook. Just scan below or visit 831stories.com/exitlane.

ACKNOWLEDGMENTS

Thank you to Claire and Erica for wondering if I just might have a romance novel in me and to Kia Thomas and Sanjana Basker for your thoughtful edits.

Thank you to my brilliant writing teachers: Allie Rowbottom, Chelsea Hodson, and Jenny Boully. And to the best parts of Bennington: Caro Claire Burke and Tamara Hilmes.

Thank you to Personal Choice, my heartbeat in LA, and Brain Trust, my sounding board in NY.

Thank you to my best friend, Ruby Smith, for the hours spent workshopping stories across from each other on the sofa for the past decade.

Thank you to my siblings/cousin, Grant, Sarah, and Ashley Veurink, for your support, long phone calls, and playlists.

Thank you to my late father, Gailen Veurink, for the fifteen years of love and encouragement that'll inspire an entire lifetime of writing. And to my mom for transcribing

ACKNOWLEDGMENTS

my first ever book and for being just as supportive of my writing now as when I was two.

Thank you to my darling husband, Christian, for everything.

ABOUT THE AUTHOR

ERIKA VEURINK is a writer, founder of EV Salon, and brand consultant who lives in Brooklyn by way of Iowa. She has an MFA from Bennington College and is a contributor to *Vogue*, *New York Magazine*, *WSJ*, and *GQ*. She writes the fashion newsletter *Long Live*. *Exit Lane* is her debut novella.

ALSO FROM 831 STORIES

Big Fan by Alexandra Romanoff
A high-profile scandal derailed Maya's DC career, and she's eager to fly under the radar—that is, until her former boy-band crush reaches out with a job offer.

Hardly Strangers by A.C. Robinson
One night with a rock star could upend Shera's best-laid plans, revealing how a chance encounter can rewrite a story—and change everything.

Comedic Timing by Upasna Barath
Naina is seeking a fresh start in NYC after breaking up with her girlfriend, but when she meets someone at a party, he's so offtype that her attraction to him fuels an identity crisis.

Set Piece by Lana Schwartz
When a breakout BBC star gets swarmed by fans during a night out, it's a no-nonsense bartender, CJ, who rescues him—and warms them both up for an after-hours hookup.

Square Waves by Alexandra Romanoff
The first spin-off in the *Big Fan* series, an enemies-to-lovers romance in which tabloid fodder mixes with a long-brewing rivalry as Cassidy contends with her high-school nemesis.

831 STORIES BOOK CREDITS

So many people were involved in bringing this book to life. Many of their names are included here, but there would be no HEA without the passionate work of booksellers and librarians and the enthusiasm of readers. And as we all know, romance readers are the best readers.

831 Stories
Erica Cerulo, Marie Joh, Catherine Krenzer, Claire Mazur, Angela Vang

Authors Equity
Andrea Bachofen, JoliAmour Dubose-Morris, Rose Edwards, Ilana Gold, Carly Gorga, Sarah Christensen Fu, Deb Lewis, Madeline McIntosh, Nina von Moltke, Kathleen Schmidt, Diana Simmons, Erin Vandeveer, Don Weisberg, Craig Young

831 STORIES BOOK CREDITS

C47 Design
Phil Chang, Haneu Kang, Jamin Lee, Naomi Otsu, Sunny Park

Editing
Sanjana Basker, Kia Thomas

Marketing, Events, and Publicity
Emma Benshoff, Tara Larsen, Ashleigh Magee, Elaine Orihuela, Kaitlin Phillips, Riley Vaske, Kristin White

Production
Sam Martin at Scribe Inc.

Keep reading for a taste of

Set Piece

by Lana Schwartz

from 831 Stories

Jack

On a small phone screen, I watch as a woman with almond-shaped eyes sticks her head out of the window of her posh Marylebone flat.

"Are you mad? Come out of the rain already," she calls out.

Then, the camera switches perspective.

A man stands in the street below. His white button-down shirt is drenched, revealing the outline of his chest and arms.

"I told you—I'm not going in there. You're coming out here," he yells back, undeterred by the fat drops of rain falling from the sky.

One of my hands goes to my face while the other moves to cover the phone screen, as if driven by instinct for self-preservation.

"Hey!" my mate George cries out next to me, shoving my palm off his phone. "I'm watching that!"

I feel my cheeks redden. Drawing my hand away is like fighting a losing battle with myself.

"It's *my* party, and I still haven't seen it." Tom reaches for the phone now, and George happily obliges.

"Alright, *alright*," I say, relenting and returning my hand to its rightful place—splayed across my eyes—so I won't

LANA SCHWARTZ

have to see the action unfold in front of me. Suddenly, this dimly lit dive bar doesn't feel nearly dark enough.

The thing is, I don't need to see the phone to know what's about to happen between the woman and man on the screen because *I* am the man on the screen.

The woman, now giving into the man's demands, bursts out of her pastel-pink Victorian town house and flings herself into his arms. They kiss in the middle of the abandoned street, engulfed in each other and enraptured by the other's lips, teeth, and tongue. The man hoists the woman up by her hips and carries her, kissing still, across the threshold of her flat. He tosses her on the bed and stands over her.

He pulls her shirt over her head, then her skirt down her legs. Turning his attention to his own clothes, he feverishly unbuttons his shirt before tugging down his pants. Music soars in the background. He steps out of his trousers, then his boxers, revealing his giant, erect—

"OK," I say, snatching the phone out of Tom's grip. "That's enough."

Sitting there while my mates watch me act is bad enough, but being present for their reactions to the much-talked-about sex scene in the BBC show I costarred in and thought all of five people would see . . .

"Oh, come on. This is some of your finest work!" George laughs. "Jack Felgate's *biggest* role to date." He gives me a devilish grin.

I roll my eyes. "Yeah, well, tonight is about Tom."

Tom pushes his Clark Kent glasses up the bridge of his nose. "I'm perfectly fine with tonight being about you.

SET PIECE

Consider this your punishment for running off to settle the bill."

"Please. What kind of friend would I be if I let you pay the tab for your own stag party?"

"And you know he can afford it now," George quips. "Unlike the rest of us poor thespians."

I blush again. It's true, but I don't want to admit it.

"Next location?" I suggest, pulling Tom to his feet.

He stumbles slightly as he stands, and I take his tipsiness as a win. I worried when he insisted on a quiet celebration near his home in Pasadena with only a small group—the trio of us actors who'd met in London, plus his brother, Jim, and his future brother-in-law, Teddy—that he was keeping it low-key for my benefit. As grateful as I am that he's avoided the kind of weekend that could land me in the pages of the *Daily Mail* and give everyone another reason to talk, I want him to have a true night out.

"You good, mate?" I grip Tom's elbow as we head to the door.

"I am absolutely peachy." Tom taps my cheek. "I want you to know, Jack, that I am really, really proud of you."

"Thank you, Tom." He, George, and I met doing theater in uni, and over the last few years, they both felt that westward tug toward Los Angeles, leaving me by my lonesome in London. For a while, we were always up for the same roles, yet we somehow managed to keep a sense of humor if one of us nabbed it over the other.

"Don't tell George," he says in a stage whisper as we exit toward a hulking Uber, "but I always knew that you were going to be the famous one out of all of us. I read that script for *Flames Flickie Flick Flicker . . .*"

"*Flames Flicker Eternal.*"

"Yes. That one—and I knew that this one's special."

When I got the script for *Flames Flicker Eternal*—or *Flames*, as the fans now call it—I could sense there was something different about it. Production had already attached a British theater director known for her quiet, intimate plays with searing dialogue and an Oscar-nominated cinematographer with a flair for the romantic. But still, even the best BBC fare often flies under Americans' radar. I never expected that Netflix would pick it up. Or that its streaming debut would coincide with a February snowstorm in the Northeast that kept everyone at home for five days. Suddenly, what started as buzz about this clandestine love story reached a full-on frenzy that could not be ignored. My inbox was bursting with media opportunities and interview requests, and so was my costar Ginny's. Four months later, I'm getting offers without auditions, and for the first time in five years, my agent is paying me more good-news calls than she is sending "they went in another direction" emails.

As we make our way to our next location, our voices volley around the car, debating whether Man United can keep its edge over Liverpool. My phone buzzes from my jeans pocket, alerting me that I have too many emails to return and at least four missed calls from my team. It can wait. All of it.

"Ay, we're here," Teddy calls out from the front seat.

"What? Already?" I ask. We've been in the car for less than ten minutes. "Couldn't we have just walked?"

SET PIECE

Everyone laughs. The driver most loudly.

"Welcome to Los Angeles," George says, swinging open the door.

My three previous trips had all been in service of bit parts, the kind of stuff I booked before *Flames Flicker Eternal* that barely justified the jet lag it brought on. I'd film all day and then retreat to whatever hotel I was being put up in near the set, my meals craft services or room service.

As I lead the charge and enter the redbrick building with the words Swan Dive hand-painted on the door, I take in the change of scenery: marble bar, art deco furnishings, and proper glassware in every hand. Despite the name, a dive this is not.

"Is that Jack Felgate?" a woman wearing a slip dress and holding a coupe whispers as we pass.

"*No way*," another whispers back. "He lives on a shire in England. Or something."

I look toward the bar, then back out at the group. *How can I get out of this?*

"Why don't we skip this one and move on to the next?" Tom throws me a life raft. As always.

"No, no, no." I shake my head. I can't let my hang-ups get in the way of Tom's good time.

Besides, I have a contingency plan. I knew I needed to prepare for the possibility I might be recognized. It's started to happen since the show came out. My favorite pub tipped off a paparazzo that I was a regular at Thursday night trivia, and pictures of me leaving were splattered across the internet. By the next week, trivia was mobbed with fans asking for selfies, and when I ran out of the bar panicked, onlookers told news outlets that I was rude and "too big for my britches." My first girlfriend shared with *The Sun* that she always knew I would make it. My year seven teacher gave an interview about what sort of student I was ("well-mannered" and "attentive"—in other words: unremarkable). Getting offers for roles with actors and directors I've dreamed of working with is thrilling. The rest of it is not.

I reach into my bag for a pair of fake glasses I'd grabbed at the pharmacy and a red beanie. It's June, but that hardly matters in Los Angeles.

"What the fuck is that?" George sizes me up in confusion. "Jesus Christ, man. Is that a *disguise*?"

Tom squints. "You look like Where's Wally."

"Worry about yourselves, yeah? Let's just go into the bar." I scan the crowd as we enter. Maybe those women were an aberration. Or everyone is just far too cool to care: This city is crawling with celebrities far bigger and more important than me. I clock an attractive bartender efficiently mixing drinks and fitting right in with the good-looking patrons.

My shoulders relax as we make our way to an empty table.

Until a woman steps in front of me, blocking my path. She's holding her iPhone, boasting a picture of a dog as white and fluffy as a cloud, inches from my face.

I hear her asking, fuzzy and as if through water, "You're Jack Felgate, aren't you? Will you take a picture with me?"

I force my vision to zoom out. The phone is connected

SET PIECE

to a hand, which is connected to an arm, which belongs to the voice asking me to confirm my identity. This is one of the women from before. Her eyes are wide. Frozen in place, I nod slowly.

"Bitch! I *told* you it was him!" she calls out to her friends, who rush over to join her. Their phones come at me as quickly as their questions do.

"Why are you wearing glasses? Do you wear glasses?"

"What are you doing *here*?"

"You *changed* my life in *Flames*. Did you know that?"

"Oh my God, you *cannot* be here. Do you come here all the time?"

"Will you *please* take a picture with us?"

I weigh my options and try to keep my expression placid. If I refuse to take photos, I will hurt their feelings, and I'll be branded a bad sport. But if I agree to, well, when does it stop?

I stand there, immobile, unable to make up my mind. My tongue is thick and heavy, my mouth dry.

"Hey! The private room you requested is ready and waiting for you." The bartender has left her post from behind the bar and is by my side. Her golden waves are stacked on top of her head, and she's wearing a simple black T-shirt and a pair of vintage-looking jeans that hang from her hips.

"Oh, sorry we're late. Ran into a bit of traffic," I say, regaining sensation in my mouth and my limbs, like I'm coming down from an allergy attack.

"Well, come on." She nods to me before turning to the

throng. "We're charging this man an exorbitant amount of money—I have to get him back there." She is both conspiratorial and firm.

As the first woman who approached me opens her mouth to object, the bartender continues, adjusting her hair. "And, of course, a round of drinks on the house for you ladies for being so accommodating."

The women exchange glances, and after about thirty seconds, it appears a consensus is reached. Their phones go back into purses, and I follow hot on my rescuer's trail.

"Is there really a back room?" I ask, hurrying closer to her.

"Please." She turns to look back at me. "I am a woman of my word."

She flashes me a bright smile, and my fingertips prickle in excitement.

"You're in luck," she says, punching in a door code. "Leo and Toby canceled last minute." She gestures for me to enter, and I know I'm supposed to take in the VIP grandeur of it, offer faint praise, at the very least. But I can't stop my eyes from landing on her.

The swath of her tan collarbone just visible at the neck of her shirt. The tiny diamond studs in her ears, somehow both sophisticated and no-nonsense. Her defined arms, strong . . . I want to know what from. Everything about her seems purposeful and controlled, except for her hair. She radiates gravitas—and also a warmth that suggests her skin would be hot to the touch. When she smiles again, her soft brown eyes crinkle with amusement, as if there is more she's holding back, and I want to know that too.

SET PIECE

"Seriously? Leo and Toby?" I ask, remembering where I am.

"Well, no." She laughs. "But we did have a last-minute cancellation. It's all yours. I'll round up your friends."

"Let me give you my card."

"We can settle up at the end of the night." Her eyes search mine, and we both stand there a beat longer than is natural. Like she might be keen on me too.

"What's your name?" she asks.

So she doesn't recognize me.

"Jack Felgate. And you?"

"Cara."

I hold out my hand, and she put hers in mine. I shake it slowly. I was right. Her skin sets mine on fire.